Walk Through a Window

A
Walk
Through a
Window

—ɯ—

kc dyer

Doubleday Canada

Doubleday Canada and colophon are trademarks

LIBRARY AND ARCHIVES CANADA CATALOGUING IN PUBLICATION
Dyer, K. C
    A walk through a window / K.C. Dyer.
ISBN 978-0-385-66637-4
    I. Title.
PS8557.Y48W35 2009   jC813'.6   C2008-906952-8

This book is a work of fiction. Names, characters, places and incidents are products of the author's imagination or are used fictitiously. Any resemblance to actual events or locales or persons, living or dead, is entirely coincidental.

Text design: Andrew Roberts
Printed and bound in the USA

Published in Canada by Doubleday Canada,
a division of Random House of Canada Limited

Visit Random House of Canada Limited's website: www.randomhouse.ca

10 9 8 7 6 5 4 3

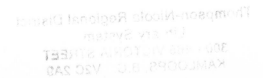

For Irene Jean Forsythe
&
Maurice Ferno Graves

With memories of love . . .
and porridge.

There isn't any one Canada,
any average Canadian,
any average place, any type.

—Miriam Chapin,
They Outgrew Bohemia (1960)

Prologue

Gabe was no longer standing by the tree. Instead he'd stepped up onto the windowsill.

"What are you doing?" she whispered.

Even though she knew.

He reached up and ran his fingers along the stones of the sill. "No loose rocks here," he said, and held out his hand.

She stared at his hand and felt the air hum.

"I will stay by your side," he said softly.

She couldn't help herself. Her stomach clenched—with excitement or fear or . . . she didn't know what.

"I have to be back to help Nan with supper," she said, stepping up beside him.

"You'll be back," he said, and she felt his warm hand around her cold fingers as they stepped through the window together.

Chapter One

Escape was clearly the only option.

"This is the wrong address," Darby said to the cab driver. "Just take me back to the airport—I'll figure something out there."

"I'm sorry, dear," the driver said apologetically, and gestured at the scrap of paper clipped to his dashboard. "I've been given strict instructions to drop one Miss D. Christopher at this here address. And if I know Etta, she'd be mighty upset with me if I misplaced her granddaughter."

Great. Darby stared glumly out the window at the scene unfolding outside. "You know my Nan?"

The cab driver popped the trunk and heaved himself out of the car. "Everyone knows your nan, kiddo. She's a good sport. So's your grandpa."

Darby didn't budge. From the cab window she watched as a woman with vivid red hair stepped up and placed her hand on the shoulder of some guy operating a ladder on a fire truck. Even from inside the cab Darby could see the way the woman's lips pinched together.

She was talking to Ladder Guy. After a few words he nodded and yelled up to his partner. The bucket lowered with a jerk, the woman stepped inside and the contraption rose up to near the top of the tree.

Bad enough to be stuck in some little one-lobster town for the summer. Bad enough to have to fly here as an unaccompanied minor in a cattle car disguised as an airplane. Bad enough that no one bothered to show up to meet the plane. But when the taxi pulled up in front of Darby's grandparents' house it was hard to decide which was worse: a man she had never met perched high in the branches of an old oak tree, or the crowd below, as they laughed, chatted and cheered on the fireman in his cherry picker, trying to talk the old coot down.

Darby recognized Gramps from a couple of old pictures that her dad kept in a bottom drawer. She'd never met either of her grandparents in person—at least as long as she could remember. Nan had to be one of the grey-haired ladies waiting at the bottom of the ladder. She hadn't seen her face yet, mostly because Darby didn't want to meet anyone's eye. Why any of this was happening was a mystery. She could feel her face flaming.

The cab driver opened the door and offered his hand to help Darby out. She ignored it, grabbed her backpack and stepped onto the street. It must have rained earlier, and one of her new white runners splashed square into a rusty puddle by the curb.

Great.

"Was trying to help you avoid that," muttered the driver, as he stalked around the back of the vehicle.

Darby thought about getting mad at this, but the truth was the scene in the front yard had used up all her available emotions at the moment.

She felt the cabbie's hand on her shoulder. "Yer grandpa is just having everyone on, Missy. The man has a sense of humour that's funny as a three-dollar bill."

She shook off his hand and forced herself to look around the crowd of people. The two grey-haired women stood out from the rest. While everyone else chattered and laughed, they stayed put right near the truck, watching the other lady take her trip up in the cherry picker. Darby took a deep breath, shouldered her pack and headed over.

At the treetop, the red-haired woman was having more luck than Ladder Guy. She had barely said two words before the old man was reaching his hand out to grasp the side of the bucket. He stepped smartly into the cherry picker just like it had been his plan all along.

Ladder Guy steered the bucket down and Darby's grandfather waved to the cheering crowd as they descended. The shadows began to lengthen and people started to wander away.

One of the old women on the ground embraced the red-haired woman as she stepped out of the cherry picker, so Darby headed for the other one.

"Excuse me," she said, but the woman did not appear to hear. Darby repeated herself a bit louder.

The lady finally heard Darby and turned in surprise. "Goodness gracious!" she said, peering up into her face. "This must be wee Darby!"

Since the girl was taller by about three inches, Darby felt she could have safely dropped the "wee" part. Sheesh. The lady looked over at the cab. The taxi driver had walked over to shake hands with the crazy old man and both of them were laughing uproariously.

"We've been expecting you, dear," she said, and immediately began rummaging in the giant vinyl bag that dangled from her arm. "Ernie will need his fare. Let me just look after it, now that all the excitement is over." She scurried across and thrust some money at the driver who doffed his hat.

"Thank you kindly, Helen. That'll do nicely." Darby could hear his radio crackle from the depths of his car. He gave a final slap on the shoulder to the star of the show and slammed himself back into his cab before slowly coasting off down the street.

The old lady scurried across the grass and gave Darby another thorough looking-over before clutching her by the arm. Her eyes narrowed and her mouth tightened a little.

"Quite an arrival time you've chosen," she said. "Hasn't been this much excitement since someone tried to blow up the legislature a few years ago."

Great. Nothing like a grandparent whose antics compare to a terrorist act.

Still clutching Darby's arm, she turned to holler across the lawn. "Look who I've got here, Etta!" she crowed. The red-haired woman snapped her head around.

As soon as Darby saw the red-haired woman's face up close, she knew her. She looked just like Darby's dad, except shorter, wrinklier and female, of course.

"Helen," she said to the lady who was still gripping Darby like a prize tuna, "did you pay Ernie for his drive from the airport?"

Great, thought Darby. *We haven't even met yet, and I'm already a financial burden.*

"There's no need for that, I'm sure," she said, when Helen bobbed her head. "Now take this, and thank you for your kindness."

She pressed money into Helen's palm and turned to face Darby, taking the girl's shoulders in her hands and gazing at her from arm's length.

"So this is the Darby-girl at last." For the first time a smile broke through the worry on her face. "I meant to meet you at the airport, but as you can see, my plans changed a little." She brushed her hands off briskly. "Excitement's all over, my dear. Let's get you inside and settled, shall we?"

"But . . ." Darby looked over at the old man, still beaming and shaking hands with well-wishers.

"Ach, never mind your grandfather right now, love. I'll see to him presently."

Nan bustled off, muttering something about dinner being charred beyond recognition. The fire truck honked once as it pulled away from the curb, and Darby reached down to grab her suitcase from where Ernie had left it on the front porch.

The scent of dinner wafted through a window. In spite of Nan's worry, nothing smelled burned, but Darby didn't feel hungry in the slightest. As she straightened up with her suitcase, she found Gramps standing with a hand on the porch rail. He'd stopped laughing.

7

"Last saw you when you were ten days old," he said. "Ye've grown a bit."

What else did he expect? Darby didn't know what to say—so she settled on saying nothing at all.

"Best come in for your supper—don't want to keep your Nan waiting," he said, at last. "Some fool's held her up enough already." He gestured at the retreating lights of the fire truck. "Those boys'd better sharpen their eyes if they're looking for a blaze. No fire around here, far's I can see." He stumped up the two steps to the front door and Darby watched it slap closed behind him.

"Welcome to Charlottetown," she muttered, and wrestled her bags inside.

—m—

9:40 p.m. Darby lay in bed and flicked her watch light on and off.

9:41 p.m. She'd been in this time zone for less than four hours and it sure didn't feel like bedtime. At home she'd just be flipping on her Xbox to play her favourite Tony Hawk skateboard game.

9:42 p.m. This was going to be one long summer.

After supper, Nan had promised to take Darby into town the next day. Then she had shown her around the house. Darby would be staying in her dad's old room, up a set of back stairs at the top of the house. It had been hot up there earlier, but Nan had opened the window and the night air had cooled the room down a bit. The old folks' room was downstairs, so she had a bit of privacy, anyhow. And, as it seemed unlikely Nan would hike up the stairs again that night, she flipped the bedside light back on. It wasn't that she was scared of the dark or anything; she just felt like a little light, that's all.

It seemed pretty obvious Nan hadn't changed a thing in the room since Darby's dad had lived there. His golf trophies were all lined up on a couple of high shelves. There was a poster on one slanted wall of a bunch of guys with electric guitars and huge hair. A rickety old desk was pushed over to the other side where the ceiling came down low. The room was right under the roof, so there was really only one wall and that had the door in it. The ceiling tilted sharply down on either side, leaving just enough space for the bed and desk.

Darby had unpacked her stuff into the desk drawers since there wasn't a dresser. She didn't have much anyway. Mostly bathing suits and shorts—and one of the geeky knitted sweaters that Nan sent every Christmas. Like she'd ever wear it. Darby figured her mother had just packed it so Nan might see it and consider it a regular part of her wardrobe.

As if.

The only good thing about the room was a window that jutted out. There was an old-fashioned kind of window seat beside it. It had a grotty old cushion covered in hunting dogs and wheat sheaves, but it was pretty comfortable all the same. Darby slid out of bed and padded the two steps it took to get there, careful not to make a noise that would let Nan know she was up.

From her spot at the window Darby could see the

whole backyard, though it was pretty hard to pick out much in the dark. There were tons of stars—way more than she had ever seen in Toronto. Good thing, too, because they lit up the yard a bit. You never really know what's out there if it's pitch black.

Darby had talked to her mom on the phone after supper. She was full of the sort of fake cheerfulness that made Darby really crazy.

"We're working hard trying to get the new house settled, darling," her mother had said. "But we're facing a few challenges. You are so lucky to be in PEI. The beaches! The sunshine! You must be having such a great time already!"

Darby had tried to remind her that she'd only been here for a few hours. Plus, from what she could see, the beaches were not very close and the old folks didn't drive. But her mom just ignored her and put her dad on the line. He told Darby the house reno was a disaster—her mom must have forgotten to coach him on fake cheeriness.

When Darby complained about the beaches, he said, "Take the bus. You're an independent kid. In my day we had to walk everywhere. I know you'll figure it out."

Thanks, Dad. Whatever you say.

Neither of them got her hints about Gramps and his little episode in the tree. The kitchen phone was really old with a short cord, and Darby couldn't exactly tell them the whole story with the two oldies sitting there at the table listening. But come on. Nan and Gramps are Dad's parents after all. How could he not see he'd sent Darby to a loony bin?

"Always looking on the dark side. Dark-side Darby."

She could hear her mother's voice, clear as a bell. Her mother said it all the time. Except this time, her mom was five provinces away. Five provinces away from the embarrassment of a grandfather who had spent the afternoon at the top of a tree.

9:47 p.m. Not even a TV in the stupid room. Nothing for Darby to do but drag her sorry butt back into bed. The lamp on the bedside table had a little golfer holding up the shade. Beside it was a new blue notebook. She pulled it onto her lap and worked the pen out from its spot in the coiled spine. On the last day of school—only two days ago, even though it seemed a lot longer—Darby and her classmates had been introduced to their teacher for the upcoming term. They'd met for only a few minutes, but even in that short time she could tell grade eight was going to be a real winner of a year.

Darby had never seen the teacher before. She must be new. She acted all excited and keen and wrote her name on the board in all capital letters. MS. AERIE. More like MIS-ERY. It was totally depressing.

She'd walked around the class and put a paper on every desk. Darby's friend Sarah made a face from across the room. They couldn't sit together because the new teacher had alphabetized the seats. Obviously the world would end if a Christopher sat next to a Slivowitz. As soon as Darby read the paper, she knew what Sarah's face had meant. Unbelievable. Homework? Over summer?

"It's just a little journal," the new teacher chirped. "No more than a daily paragraph or two at most. Just tell me about your summer. You'll be so happy that you did."

Brandon Harris made a gagging noise behind Darby, and immediately about five of his friends copied him. It had tickled Darby to see the way Ms. Aerie's face fell, but in the end she was tougher than she looked. "We'll start the new year with a pizza party if all the journals are completed," she said. Yeah, like that would make a difference.

Darby had planned to conveniently forget the whole thing, but it turned out the new teacher had sent an email to all the parents, too. Her mom had the blue notebook waiting when she got home.

Sitting up in her dad's old bed in Charlottetown, Darby had to admit she did sort of like a new notebook. All those fresh pages. The promise of something new without the lame scribbles and scratches of actual work.

She grabbed a pen and drew a flower on the first page. Hey, it was a start. But there was no way she was going to describe meeting her grandparents. She'd be the laughing stock of the school if *that* got around.

She was just considering actually hauling out some pencil crayons from her backpack when she heard something scratch the door.

Darby suddenly remembered she was alone at the top of some old house in a place she'd never been before.

Her blood froze.

Okay, maybe that's not possible. But she was sure her heart stopped or missed a beat or something before it started up again, pounding like a jackhammer in her ears.

It's not that she was scared of the dark, or anything. It's just that there was no light in the tiny little staircase that led to her room. It was one old, dark stairwell.

Whatever it was scratched the door again. Darby sat there quivering in bed, hoping like mad that one of the old folks would hear the noise and come and investigate. Even a flashlight coming up the stairs would push back some of the suffocating blackness on the other side of the bedroom door.

"Who do you think you are kidding?" she whispered to herself. "Those old people are downstairs snoring while I'm up here dealing with some kind of weird Creature of the Dark." But the sound of her own voice seemed so loud, she clapped one hand over her mouth and stared at the door, eyes wide with horror.

She was on her own.

In the corner by the desk was her dad's old putter. Better than nothing. Her feet felt like they had cement in them, but the element of surprise was all she had.

She managed to grab the golf club and swing open the door in one fast move.

Gramps was standing there with a knife in his hand.

Darby screamed, something jumped at her and adrenaline took over.

She swung that putter like a PGA Tour veteran. Unfortunately, all she connected with was one of her dad's trophies on a shelf over the door, and it shattered to smithereens. But, in the end, it was okay.

Because, of course, Nan was right behind Gramps in the hall. The knife turned out to be a can opener. And after everything settled down a bit, it seemed the one family member Darby hadn't yet met was a calico cat named Maurice.

At least Nan had brought up a flashlight.

It took a whole lot of yelling and yowling, but things finally started to come clear. Gramps assured Darby that he was just trying to lure the cat downstairs with the can opener, and Nan told her she was tired of dusting that old trophy, anyhow. The cat curled up on Darby's bed and acted as though nothing out of the ordinary had happened.

It was a long time after the old folks had headed back down the stairs before she was able to even think about sleep. She'd been scared—no denying it. It must have taken an hour for her heart rate to go back to normal.

But Darby had also seen the look on Gramps's face in the instant she flung open the door. He'd looked more frightened than she was. And he looked lost. Lost in his own house.

The cat curled at her feet and purred himself to sleep. But sleep wouldn't come for Darby. Instead, a wave of homesickness washed over her.

She closed her eyes and tried to talk herself out of her loneliness and into sleep. She had survived her first day of the visit to Charlottetown. She'd taken her first solo airplane trip. And Gramps had made it safely out of the tree. It had been a pretty weird first day of summer. Not really a comforting sort of day, all in all. She decided to leave her light on to keep any more weirdness from closing in. But it was still a long time before sleep claimed her.

Afterward, Darby often thought it was probably a good thing she hadn't known just how much weirder things were going to get.

Chapter Two

The next morning, Gramps made porridge for breakfast. Apparently this was what he ate every day. He slapped down a bowlful in front of Darby, along with a pitcher of milk and a look that dared her to say something. She thought about refusing to eat it, but when he shot a second glance over his shoulder, she reconsidered.

That porridge had to be about the worst thing Darby had ever tasted. Gloopy didn't even begin to describe it. The first bite tasted like she'd chewed it up, spat it out and chewed it a second time. Choking it down was going to be a problem. She decided to wait it out. He had to leave the room sooner or later, and the window into the garden was temptingly near.

Gramps dropped a bowl onto the place mat beside hers and sat down with a grunt. "This stuff'll stick to your ribs, kiddo," he said, and glanced into her bowl.

She scooped a small spoonful up and tried to avoid his eye.

He stood up with a snort of disapproval. But when he sat down, the sugar bowl landed in front of Darby with a thump. "See if that'll help it slide down a little easier," he said.

Three heaping tablespoons of brown sugar went a long way toward making the porridge more edible. And Gramps was right—Darby could normally knock back a couple of bowls of cereal in the morning, or at least three pieces of toast, but after that porridge there wasn't room for anything else.

Maurice wound around her ankles as she ate. Gramps scowled before getting up to pour food into the cat dish.

"Ye should be earning y'er living eating rodents, ye walking fuzzball."

As the cat bent to eat, Gramps stroked the soft back surreptitiously before returning to his own breakfast.

"Where's Nan?" Darby asked, as she scraped the last of the sugar and milk out of the bottom of her bowl.

"Going to town," Gramps muttered. "Better be right quick with the dishes if you want to go with her." He pointed at the sink. "You wash, I'll dry."

Darby looked around the sunny blue and white kitchen and noticed for the first time that there wasn't a dishwasher. Gramps was already filling the sink with hot water. He tossed a pair of yellow gloves at her. "Better wear those, kiddo. No good washing dishes unless the water's hot."

He wasn't joking. But since she didn't want to sit around the house all day, Darby dipped her yellow rubber hands into the scalding water and scrubbed. Gramps wiped off the counters. "When I started with the Forces, my sergeant always said to leave the place cleaner than you found it," he said, snapping the cloth in the air after he'd rinsed it.

"Your sergeant?"

He kept talking as though he hadn't heard her. "Yep—cleaner than a whore's teakettle."

"That will be enough of that kind of talk, Vern." Nan bustled into the kitchen, took the cloth from Gramps and hung it from the tap. "Ready, Darby?"

The girl nodded, thrust her gloves at Gramps and scurried out the door after Nan. She sure could move fast for an old lady.

Darby scooped up her skateboard as she headed out the back door, but Nan would have none of it.

"Not when you are walking with me, young lady."

"But Nan—it will help me to keep up with you," she pleaded.

"Leave it on the front porch, dear. You can play with it when we come back."

Sheesh. A person doesn't *play* with a skateboard. A person *rides* a skateboard. But Nan didn't look any more open for an argument than Gramps did with his porridge.

Darby tossed the board onto the front step and ran to catch up. Nan was headed down toward the end of the street. Where the pavement stopped, she turned into a small lane that ran behind an old house, its paint a chipped and faded cornflower blue. It was the last house at the end of the street.

"The houses here look pretty different from home," Darby said, as they walked into the lane. "I've never seen any of that frilly stuff around the windows before."

Nan smiled. "It's called gingerbread trim," she said. "It was very popular on houses at the turn of the century."

Something about the look of the decrepit old house told Darby she wasn't talking about the twenty-first century.

"It's a special old place," Nan continued. "Your dad used to climb those trees in the orchard back there."

Darby peered through the hedge. Sure enough, she could see a cluster of trees covered in little green apples growing beside a small structure with its roof half gone.

"Dad climbed trees?" Darby couldn't picture her dad climbing anything other than a corporate ladder.

"Yes he did. He loved eating the crab apples, though I don't know how he managed it when they are so sour. And your grandfather used to paddle him for it, too. The house wasn't in the family anymore and your father was trespassing."

Trespassing? That was even better than climbing trees. Darby began to wish she'd brought her notebook. Some of this stuff might be helpful to leverage homework time when she got home.

"Did you see that little stone building in the back?" asked Nan.

Darby nodded. "Is it an old barn?"

Nan smiled. "Your grandfather's family used it for a chicken coop, I believe. But it was originally a tiny chapel. It was entirely built of stone, apart from the wooden roof. It caught fire many years ago, so of course it's just a ruin these days."

Nan turned the corner and the leafy lane led out onto the main street. Darby followed, puffing only a little.

"So the house used to belong to our family?" she probed.

"Yes, dear, but it was sold off when your grandfather was a baby. He was born there, but his mother died very young and his father just couldn't live with the memories around the place, I guess. They moved over to the other side of town." Nan laughed a little. "I used to tease your grandfather that he just married me to get back onto Forsyth Street."

Darby followed her grandmother through the open door of the bank. "So who lives there now? It looks kinda empty."

But Nan just waved Darby over to some chairs and stepped up to speak to the clerk behind the counter. The bank clerk's voice carried clear over to where Darby was sitting.

"Lovely to see you, Mrs. Christopher. Is that your granddaughter you've brought in today?"

Nan glanced over with a smile and nodded.

"From away, then, is she not?"

From another planet, Darby thought—but Nan just beamed and said, "Toronto."

—⁓—

Turned out that Nan had a long list of errands—a *long* list. It was a hot day and the streets were busy, so when she pointed out the big library, Darby was more than ready to quit fighting the tourist crowds and get out of the sun. They agreed to meet in an hour and Darby headed inside to see about getting herself a library card.

"Behave as if I were watching you," Nan called out.

Darby snorted under her breath and hurried away. It was pure relief to get out from under those watching eyes for a while.

The library was inside the big Confederation building downtown. Darby looked around. One thing she'd already learned in less than twenty-four hours on Prince Edward Island was that the people seemed really proud of two things—Anne of Green Gables and Confederation. But as far as she was concerned, the tourists could keep Anne, and she didn't care a bit what historical event the building was commemorating. It was nice and cool inside and that made her happy.

It took only a few minutes at the counter before Darby had her new library card. As she started to walk toward the geography section, a woman who was working nearby reached out and touched her shoulder. Darby jumped about a foot in the air.

"I'm sorry to bother you," the woman said, "but I thought I heard you say your name was Christopher."

"I did," said Darby, warily. She wasn't used to strangers strolling up to talk from out of the blue. In her experience, they were usually asking for money, so she spent a lot of time trying to look the other way, given the lame amount of allowance she got.

"Well, you must be Darby, then! Etta told me she was expecting you this week."

Darby's mouth dropped open a little in surprise. Either her Nan was a serious mouthpiece, or the people around here had nothing better to do than to snoop into other folks' business.

The lady laughed at the look on Darby's face and set down the poster she'd been attaching to the wall. "My name is Shawnie Stevens. You know the yellow house beside your grandma's? That's where I live."

Aha. So Nan was a big talker after all.

"Nice to meet you," Darby said, automatically. She searched her memory, but couldn't recall Shawnie's face from the crowd at the bottom of the tree the day before. She had a strong, square jaw and her hair was pulled into a long thick braid that reached down her back. Darby thought maybe she'd gotten lucky and just met the one person in town who had missed Gramps's foolishness.

"I would love it if you would bring your grandma over for tea sometime," Shawnie said, her voice so quiet Darby had to lean forward to hear her. "I've been meaning to have her over for quite a while, but my husband and I have been very busy getting ready for this show." She gestured at the poster draped over the chair.

"Mi'kmaq Cultural Event," Darby read out loud.

"It's pronounced more like *Mig-Maw* than *Mic-Mack*," Shawnie replied. "My husband and I are both artists, and we'll be displaying some of our work at the library this month."

The poster looked okay, but Darby had seen a lot of native artwork at home, too. This didn't look much different. She looked at the poster again. Beaver quill baskets and flowers made out of birch bark, plus a bunch of stone carvings.

"The pictures look pretty nice," Darby admitted. "Maybe I'll come to see your show."

Shawnie blushed. "That would be wonderful," she said. "Your grandma has been very supportive of my work. When you come for tea I'll show you some of the other pieces I'm working on." She picked up her poster. "See you soon, I hope," she said, and turned back to pinning it up.

We'll see about that, Darby thought. She headed off to find a book or two to make her library visit look good to Nan.

—ᴍ—

Darby left a pile of library books on the table inside the front door and grabbed her skateboard off the porch. Nan and Gramps had gone off to a doctor's appointment, so she locked the door carefully and hid the key under the garden gnome with the red hat. Time for a little practice before dinner. She needed to get her ollie more than two inches above the ground before she got back to Toronto. Lately she'd been getting so little air on her jumps it was an embarrassment.

She rolled to the end of the block downtown, but the streets were still pretty crowded. No place to really get a good glide going, and jumps were out of the question.

Boring.

Darby thought about skating down to the library, but she'd been there already. Ultraboring. The sun was really blazing, so she cruised back up Forsyth Street looking for a shady patch. Nan and Gramps's house was closed up tight—they must still be at the doctor's office.

She remembered again what Nan had said. *"Behave like*

I'm watching you." Darby sighed, and stepped off her skateboard to walk a bit. A whole summer of cautious old-lady sayings like that to look forward to. *I bet she used to say that to my dad and his brothers,* Darby thought bitterly.

She hopped back on her board and thought about practising her grind on the sidewalk. Except there was no sidewalk. In Toronto there were sidewalks along both sides of every street in her neighbourhood.

Yet another way that Charlottetown failed to measure up to home.

Darby pushed off with one foot, heading toward a shady sort of park near the end of the street. She stared at the houses as she passed them, thinking again how different they looked from the houses in Toronto. Hardly any brick, for one thing. They all looked like stupid cracker boxes standing on end. Most of them had little tiny windows and some were built right up against the street without any front yard at all. One of them even had a rusty old anchor out front.

She hadn't seen many kids around either, apart from the tourists. It seemed like an old town filled with mostly old people.

Thrilling place to spend the summer.

Darby found herself down by the old blue house at the end of the street. It definitely had an abandoned look to it. Weird to think Gramps had grown up here. Unlike most of the other places on Forsyth, this one had a pretty big front yard.

As she glided into the shady side of the street, the air chilled down almost immediately—so fast that goose bumps arose on the skin of her arms. She had a sudden sense that someone was watching. But the front door was tightly shut and the curtains were drawn against the heat of the day. And there certainly didn't seem to be anyone close by. An old rusty gate stood gaping open at the end of the front walk like an invitation. She flipped her board up with one toe and walked in.

The house itself looked pretty creepy up close. Peeling paint, broken windows—the whole haunted/possessed/scene-of-the-crime thing that reminded her of every scary movie she'd seen. Nobody had been looking after the garden, either. Compared to all the neat gardens along the street, this yard had been allowed to run wild. There were still lots of flowers, but they were spilling out of the beds and were all through the lawn, maybe seeded into the grass by the wind.

She walked around the back, her thoughts on those crab apple trees. Near the back of the lot was the old stone building that Nan had mentioned. It was in even worse shape than the main house, and Darby could see where most of the roof had caved in. Something moved in the shadows and she nearly jumped out of her skin. But when Maurice, Nan's cat, padded past, she had to laugh out loud. The cat hopped up onto the stone windowsill of the old building and Darby promised herself she'd quit watching scary movies in the future.

Besides, behind the house it was beautiful—kind of like a secret garden. Blackberries were growing wild all over the back area behind the trees. And the trees themselves were loaded with apples, all smaller than her fist. It smelled great, too. Not like dead stuff or the decay of a really old place. Just fresh and flowery and—

Almost sweet.

Darby shivered. Too much like an old witch's candy house in the fairy-tale woods. She clutched her skateboard a little tighter and retraced her steps around the house.

By the time she got to the front, she began to feel a little foolish for being so easily creeped out. Here it was a hot, otherwise boring, beautiful day. And this old house might be a good place to escape to if Gramps kept up the weird behaviour. Sheesh. Half the time he acted more like a kid than a grandfather.

Darby stopped in her tracks, and realized she had been wrong about there being no one else her age nearby.

The boy was wandering along the street in front of the house. He was wearing a red T-shirt and kicking something back and forth on the road. He had a kind of pattern going—two kicks left foot, kick right. Switch feet.

She stepped back into the shadow of the big tree at the front of the old house to watch him. She couldn't quite see what he was kicking. Was it a rock? Rubber ball? No—something the same size as a rock, but different.

The pattern shifted again, this time with a little twist. Three kicks left foot, two kicks right, toe flip. It was the toe flip that gave it away. Not a rock—a chestnut. Spiny as a sea urchin and still green with early summer.

This is supposed to be fun? The thought of having to stay in a place so boring for the whole summer made Darby groan aloud.

Red T-shirt looked a bit startled for a moment, then

he kicked the chestnut high so it sailed over the hedge at the side of the house.

"What's your problem?" he said.

Darby shrugged and stepped onto the road. She dropped her board and rolled it back and forth under one foot. "So this is what kids around here do with their time, eh? Kick chestnuts around all day? Not my idea of fun."

Red T-shirt scuffed his foot in the rusty soil along the side of the road. "I usually do it with a soccer ball," he said loftily, "but mine's flat today."

He started to walk away again but stopped abruptly and spun on one heel to look at her.

"You must be the kid staying at the Christophers' place," he said.

"How'd you know that?" It wasn't like she was hanging out in front of the house. They had to be more than a block away from her grandparents' place.

He grinned. "Oh y'know—word gets around."

Great. This was some lame small town, all right. Everybody seemed to make a hobby of sticking his or her nose into everybody else's business.

He glanced pointedly at the board under Darby's foot. "Skateboarder, eh?"

She nodded. "But I'm only here for a few weeks," she said. "Don't expect me to teach you any tricks or anything."

"Whatever." He turned to walk away and the rest of his words were cut off by the rising breeze.

Darby shivered a little. She realized it was getting a bit late and suddenly she didn't really want the conversation to end. After all, apart from Shawnie, this was the first person under sixty she'd spoken to since she had been here. And maybe talking to him would take her mind off the crushing boredom of an afternoon in this stupid little town.

"Hey—what did you say?" she yelled after him.

He kept walking with his shoulders hunched like he wasn't going to answer, but when he got to the corner, he stopped and turned. "I said, maybe when you've been here a while you'll learn to be a little friendlier."

Darby leaned onto her board and rolled forward a few feet. "What?"

But he just flashed her a grin and walked off along the laneway.

"Stupid kid," she said loudly, hoping he would hear and come back to take her up on it. Even an argument would be better than the boredom. But if he had heard, he didn't come back. Like *she* was the unfriendly one. Darby sighed a little. Even the other kids around here were stupid and boring. She gave the ground a vicious kick and shot off on her board, right down the middle of the street.

She'd glided nearly a whole block when a car came around the corner and paused to let her move to the side of the road. Darby flipped up her board to watch the car crawl safely by. At home in Toronto, a car going by meant she and her skateboard might have ended as a splintery smear on the road. But here even the cars moved slowly.

Her heart sank, but she tried to shake it off. How stupid was that? Not being mowed down by a car actually made her feel homesick? She shook her head a little and dropped her board back on the road with a clatter.

From her spot on the road, she could see the sun as it dipped slowly behind the old blue house, lighting up the gingerbread trim in a brilliant golden glow.

The sky was pink and serene, and a bird somewhere nearby twittered its evening song. The scene couldn't be tamer if it came from an oil painting on Nan's wall. She kicked off again.

Darby wasn't about to admit it, but the truth was that she couldn't actually skateboard very well. *I might be a total amateur,* she thought, *but nobody around here needs to know that, least of all some lame local kid who can't even conduct a decent conversation.*

At least she'd get a chance to work on her boarding. A single bright spot in a dismal summer forecast. Nan and Gramps's house came into sight and Darby zipped back toward it. She passed the yellow house next door—Shawnie's place, obviously. The day was shifting into twilight, clear and calm, with no sign of the earlier breeze. Lights were starting to come on up and down the street as people got home from work. She could smell a barbecue in someone's yard and her stomach rumbled a bit.

As far as Darby could tell, everything was perfectly normal on the start of another quiet evening in Charlottetown.

So why couldn't she shake the feeling that no matter how fast she rolled along, someone was following her?

Chapter Three

It took Darby until the next day to finally make it to the park she'd seen just up the street from her grandparents' house. It turned out to be—big surprise—pretty old. It was mostly filled with huge overgrown trees shading an old slide that was tilting at a dangerous angle. She found a single wooden swing suspended from the branch of a giant old chestnut tree. The ground was littered with spiky little chestnut burls like the one Red T-shirt had been kicking down the street the day before.

After breakfast, Nan had told Darby that she had a job for her to do, and that she was expected home at eleven. That gave Darby a couple of hours to practise skateboarding, which was fine by her. In fact, it fit right into Darby's new survival plan.

She might be stuck in a dead-end town for the summer, but at least she had her board. And by the time she got back to Toronto, Darby decided, she was going to have mastered all the tricks on her Tony Hawk DVD.

She flew back and forth along the street, thinking about staying on her skateboard and gliding all the way home to Toronto. Problem was, Charlottetown was on an island. Darby smiled a little, picturing herself with super-boarding powers skating across the waters of Northumberland Strait toward her home in Toronto.

Of course, she wouldn't even need superpowers. There was a bridge—the Confederation Bridge—running from Borden across the water to New Brunswick.

That had to be one big bridge. Gramps had said it was thirteen kilometres long. Darby hadn't known there was a bridge that long in the whole world.

It would make an awesome skateboard ride.

Deep in thought, she didn't notice a change in the road surface until it was too late. Her front wheel hit a rock, and the board stopped short. Darby managed to stay on her feet, but she wrenched her ankle just a little on the landing. She walked back, picked up her board and limped over to the swing, swaying gently under the big shady trees.

She sat on the swing, one toe on the skateboard at her feet. A minute's rest wouldn't hurt. Her ankle had stopped stinging already. She couldn't move much and still keep her foot on the board, but that was okay since she didn't feel like swinging anyway. If she made time to practise like this every day, she'd be an expert by the time she got home. As long as she didn't hit any more rocks.

She remembered getting the skateboard for her last birthday. There had been only a week or so left before the snow arrived, so she didn't really get any good practice time in. But as soon as spring arrived, she worked on mastering a long stretch of pavement at school, and then it was time to hit the road.

Yonge Street.

The longest street in Canada. It ran north from her house near Lawrence Avenue up through Thornhill and Richmond Hill and Aurora. Who knew how far it actually went? It was way longer than the Confederation Bridge. And one day Darby planned to skate the whole thing, hills and all. But first things first. When she got her board, her primary goal was to master the Eaton Centre. And that meant travelling Yonge Street the other way— down toward the lake.

All Darby's friends at school had done it. The good boarders said they had, anyway. Apparently the key is in the speed, though of course route planning is also essential. Darby's friend Sarah has been skateboarding since before she could walk. At least, that's what she tells everybody. Sarah said the Eaton Centre was just a matter of watching for the security guards and skating right on their tails. They'd never even know Darby was there.

Easy. According to Sarah.

Darby leaned back on the swing and looked up at the clear blue sky dappled with shadows from the leaves of the huge tree. Everything had been going according to plan for conquering the Eaton Centre, until her parents started to whisper.

She first noticed it at the dinner table. It had been some ordinary discussion about her day at school and how much homework her lame science teacher had loaded on—but somehow it ended up as a heated whispering match between the parental units. Soon the whispering progressed into an exchange of furious glares and even worse—silences. And it wasn't just at one dinner—oh, no. Once Darby had clued in, she could see the signs everywhere. Her parents would stop talking when she entered the room. Or they'd change the subject, and Darby began hearing undertones in every conversation.

I'm no idiot, she thought. *I can read the signs.* Darby had watched enough daytime TV to recognize what was happening. After all, it wasn't like she was the first kid whose parents ever split up.

But it still felt like a body blow when she found out they were dumping her with her grandparents for the summer. Not that they told her anything. As far as anyone knew, it was all about some stupid household renovation.

Sure.

Darby lay in bed the night before she left for Charlottetown and tried to imagine what it would feel like to be divorced. Would she live part-time with one parent like Sarah did with her dad? Or maybe she wouldn't even get to see her dad anymore. Caitlyn Morris, from gym class, claimed she hadn't seen her dad since she was eight.

But that wasn't the worst of it.

The worst of it was . . .

Something hit Darby on the head.

She shook herself out of the reverie and looked around. Sure enough, there was a chestnut on the ground. But where . . . ? And the feeling was back. Like someone was in the trees watching her.

The branch above her head rustled and Darby looked

up, startled. A large grey squirrel sat staring at her with bold black eyes. In both paws he held a giant chestnut.

"So it was you, was it?" she said to the squirrel, with a shaky laugh. "What is it with chestnuts in this place?"

"Maybe because they taste so good," said the squirrel.

Darby gasped. But before she could completely embarrass herself by responding to the rodent, a boy stepped out from behind the tree.

"Very funny," she blurted, trying madly not to blush at the thought of the close call. She scrambled away from the swing and flipped her skateboard into one hand.

The boy stared at her. He had curly hair—black as a raven's wing—and his blue eyes sparkled from a darkly tanned face.

"You thought the squirrel was speaking," he said, with barely contained glee.

"Did not."

"Maybe not, maybe so." He strode forward and took over Darby's spot on the swing, leaning back and pushing off hard with his legs. "It's not nice to tease people," he said in a reasonable tone. "Better to make friends."

Suddenly he stopped, planted his feet and stood up with one hand outstretched. "My name is Gabriel."

Darby stared at his hand for a minute, thinking. At least this guy was willing to talk to her, unlike Red T-shirt.

"I'm Darby," she said at last, and shook his hand quickly. His skin was cool, which was good because Darby hated sweaty hands. She snatched her skateboard up and stepped out of his way in case he decided to hop on the swing again.

"You are here only for the summer?" he asked.

Darby shrugged. "Not the whole summer, if I have anything to do with it. I'm from Toronto."

He nodded. "Myself, I have lived in this small place since I was a baby."

She looked at him doubtfully. "You don't sound like you're from here," she said. "You have a French accent."

"I speak French at home," he said, stepping away from the swing and flipping a rock from the ground onto his toe. He kicked his foot sharply and the rock sailed over his head, but before it could hit the ground he kicked it up with his other heel and it slapped neatly into the palm of his left hand.

She refused to be impressed. "You obviously don't spend enough time watching TV."

"I do not know about that," he said. "Me? I just like rocks." He held out his hand, and the rock sat smooth and flat and red on his palm.

This was turning into another bizarre conversation. Between Gramps and Red T-shirt and now this guy—man, was everyone in this town weird?

"Okay, so it's a nice rock," Darby admitted. "And it's that colour because of the iron in the soil. Everybody knows that."

The boy laughed. "Yes, the soil means there are no white dogs on the Island, for sure."

"Or white runners," she said, looking down at the rust-coloured stain on her new shoes.

Gabriel leaned back on the swing. "You can have white shoes anywhere," he said. "I think the rocks are red because they are the heart of this place. And this red island is the heart of the country."

"Oh, please." Darby rolled her eyes. "Uh, sorry Mr. Romantic Imagery, but there's no way that PEI is the heart of Canada. I live in Toronto. Have you ever been there?"

Gabriel shook his head.

"Well, it's the biggest city in the country. Millions of people all living and working in one place. Way more than live on this whole island, let alone in this stupid little town."

Darby's face started to feel hot and she was embarrassed to feel tears stinging behind her eyelids. She blinked them back and to cover up, shouted at him. "Everything is really exciting and there is so much to do. Movies and concerts and theatre and . . ."

"And?"

She grabbed the rock out of his hand and threw it across the street as hard as she could. It cracked into the high branches of an oak and crashed down to the base of the massive trunk. A few leaves fluttered to the ground.

"And, it's way better than this lame little place."

Unexpectedly, the boy didn't argue with Darby. She thought insulting his town should at least have gotten a rise out of him. But nothing. He just stared at her and picked up another rock.

"There may be more to this place than you think," he said, at last. "Many cultures have come together on this small island."

Darby swallowed the lump in her throat. Throwing the rock had helped her get control of the sudden bout of homesickness. The last thing she needed was to let some local guy see her get all teary.

"In Toronto, we have Caribana in the summer and we have the most amazing Chinatown and the Danforth has awesome Greek food. There's nothing like that here."

"I think you need to look more closely," he argued. "Look just at the people living on this street. I am Acadian, your grandparents—"

"Are from Canada," she cut him off. She wasn't going to let the conversation get around to Gramps if she could help it. "And I don't know anybody on the street, anyway." No point mentioning she had met Shawnie. Besides, Shawnie wouldn't have helped his argument anyway because with her Mi'kmaq heritage, she was just another boring Canadian.

"Why do you hate this place so much?" he asked.

Darby shrugged and looked at her watch. Time to go back and help Nan. "I don't know. It's boring. It's not like home and—"

"And?"

"And I'm an outsider, okay? Some lady in the bank today told Nan that I was from away. From away? What a laugh. This little island is a joke. It's so small you can hardly find it on a map! And yet the whole rest of the world is considered 'away'? I bet nothing exciting has *ever* happened here. I don't get why you think it's so great, anyway. You've probably never been anywhere else."

She looked at her watch again. "I've got to go."

He didn't argue, just turned to walk away. "Maybe I'll see you around sometime before you leave," he said, and a smile lit up his face as he slipped back into the trees. "I live in the blue house at the end of the street."

Darby nearly dropped her skateboard.

"Wait," she called out to him. "You mean the house with the gingerbread trim?"

But he was gone.

—m—

Two o'clock in the afternoon. The sun beat down on the back of Darby's neck and she turned her ball cap around to offer some protection. Her back itched. So did her shoulders. Picking raspberries was itchy business. Nan had given her a litre basket to fill and it seemed to be taking forever.

Some job. First she had Darby peel potatoes for an hour before lunch. While they were eating, Nan announced that Darby's job for the afternoon was to pick raspberries. *And* babysit Gramps.

This last part she didn't mention until Gramps had left to find his garden tool kit.

"Just keep an eye on him, Darby. I won't be out for very long and I just don't—"

"Want him to end up in a tree again?"

Nan looked at her coldly. "Young lady, your grandfather is a wonderful man. He has a few—er—eccentricities, but he has been a kind husband and father for many more years than you have walked this earth. Now, I'm sure everything will be just fine. I'll be back shortly."

She pushed the berry basket into Darby's hands and walked out the door with that red hair of hers practically bristling off her head.

"How ye doing there, kiddo?"

Gramps was back. He'd been rummaging around in Nan's garden shed. Darby brushed away a raspberry leaf that was stuck to her hat. "All right, I guess." She cast a wary eye at him. Seemed okay. No sign that he wanted to suddenly climb a tree, anyway.

"Hot work, pickin' berries."

Darby nodded and slapped at an insect buzzing near her ear.

"Ye gotta watch out for them blackflies, kiddo. This time o' year they pack a mean bite."

She nodded again and held up her arm to show him a dime-sized scab just below her elbow.

"I think one got me last night," she said. "It felt like a red-hot needle had jabbed into me."

Gramps reached across the raspberry cane brambles and grasped her wrist in one strong hand. Darby felt a bit startled by this, but almost immediately saw he was just holding up her arm so he could see the bite clearly.

"Yep, looks like one took a fair chunk outta you." He chuckled. "My dad used to tell me that God put blackflies on earth to improve my reflexes." He slapped his other hand on his thigh and the sound echoed off the trees like a rifle shot. "Suckers haven't bit me since I was ten."

Darby rubbed the sore spot on her arm and turned back to her basket. If she could get this job done before Nan returned she might have a chance to try to find Gabriel.

She wanted to hear how he and his family were able to live in that broken-down old place.

Gramps pulled his hat down low with a snort and shuffled off toward the house.

Now where's he going? Darby thought. *We're supposed to be doing this together.*

She dropped to her knees and kept picking. Gramps seemed fine today. It was stupid that she was forced to keep an eye on him. He seemed perfectly normal—even a little less cranky than at breakfast time when he caught her piling four spoonfuls of sugar onto her porridge.

And what if he did decide to do something wacky? Just what was she supposed to do about that? Not much a thirteen-year-old can do to stop a man the size of Gramps from climbing a tree if he wants to badly enough.

Darby checked her basket. Maybe fifteen decent berries. There were two main problems with berry picking. Half of the things seemed to have a little white worm or two curled up inside. Ugh. And the other half looked so juicy and red—and the day was so hot . . .

At this rate only one berry out of every five she picked was making it into the basket.

The screen door slammed and Gramps shuffled back across the lawn toward the garden. Good. No tree climbing yet.

He had a pile of old newspapers under his arm. "Gotta love *The Guardian*," he said. "At least this goddamn paper is good for something."

Earlier he'd been complaining bitterly about something he'd read in the paper. Nice to see his attitude had improved. He dropped half the papers on the ground in front of Darby and knelt down on the other half. "I'm going to let ye in on a little secret, kiddo," he said, his voice muffled by leaves as he stuck his head under the brambles. "The trick to picking raspberries is that ye have to be open to seeing things from a different angle."

Darby slapped at a mosquito and dropped to her knees. She stuck her head under the brambles, carefully keeping her distance from the little suckers on the leaves that wanted to sting her face and hands. The temperature dropped in the cool shade under the branches, and when she looked up, Darby could see masses of berries just ready for picking.

That Gramps. Full of surprises.

She rolled over on her back to look up at the clumps of red berries, each hanging from a slender stalk and dangling in their hundreds just above her head.

The leaves rustled and Gramps's head poked into Darby's little cave under the brambles. "Nan stakes 'em so they'll grow like this," he said with a grin. "Should speed up the job—long as you can keep a few of 'em outta yer mouth."

Darby picked like crazy for about five minutes and just like that her basket was full. She scrambled out from under the bushes to see her grandfather dusting off his knees. "Thanks, Gramps," she said gratefully. "That took no time at all."

About then she noticed his own basket was empty. He stuffed it into her free hand.

"Uh, well, kiddo, I've a powerful thirst that's just come

on," he said, glancing up at the house. "And since Etta is not available to get me a lemonade, I think I'll just pop down to the Legion for a quick sip."

Darby jumped to her feet and tried to think fast. This was exactly what Nan didn't want. "Er—Nan said you were going to—ah—keep an eye on me while she was out," she stammered.

"Ach—you're a big strong girl. Ye don't need old Gramps always hanging over yer shoulder," he said, already heading across the yard. "Besides, I'll be back long before Etta makes it home from her bridge game. Now you just get those berries picked, Allie my girl, and I'll bring home some vanilla ice cream to eat 'em with."

He closed the back gate and Darby stood staring after him with his basket still clutched in her hand, feeling foolish and trying to think if she even knew someone by the name of Allie.

Chapter Four

Luckily, Gramps had shown up at the house as promised, a few minutes before Nan walked in. He totally played it like he'd been home all afternoon, and Darby wasn't about to say anything different. She knew the smell of beer on someone's breath. Gramps had been gone for less than an hour and when he came back he didn't even smell of cigarette smoke, let alone beer.

Nan didn't seem to suspect a thing. But Darby prided herself on having a long memory. She mentally banked Gramps's little trip in the hope that it might buy her some freedom in the future. Sure enough, it paid off even sooner than she had hoped, though not in a way she would have ever expected.

The next morning at breakfast, Nan bustled around the kitchen adding items to a long list she'd written on the back of a cash register receipt. Then she announced she was going to head up Granville Street to the big grocery store in the mall.

"How are you planning to get all the way up there, Etta?" said Gramps.

"Not me, Vern," she said clearly. "We are going up by taxi. I have a long list and I'll need your help to carry the bags. Things are different around here these days with a teenage mouth to feed. We can't have our girl going hungry, now can we?"

Darby cringed. The guilt. Not only was her presence costing them more, but she was making more work for them, too.

"Do you want me to come, too?" she offered, hoping Nan would say no.

Nan looked like she was going to accept Darby's offer, when Gramps shot her a peculiar look. It took Darby a minute to realize he was winking.

"Let the kid have some time on her own, Etta. I'll help you at the store—and I'll even call up Ernie to see if he'll give us a discount fare on the trip."

Ah. So this was where Dad's cheap gene came from. Darby laughed a little to herself. Well, Gramps could be as cheap as he wanted as long as it gave her some time away from peeling potatoes or one of Nan's million other little jobs.

Nan's sharp eyes locked onto Darby as Gramps walked out of the room, jingling the change in his pocket in a cheerful way.

"Don't think for a minute that I don't know a payback when I see one, young lady," she said, without the hint of a smile. "Now, while you were enjoying your beauty sleep, I've spent the morning washing, so before you get to riding that skateboard of yours, there are sheets waiting to be hung up out back."

Darby bobbed her head in the most obedient manner she could muster. "Yes, Nan. I'll do them right now."

"See that you do." She picked up her purse and followed Gramps through the front door. "Now, Vern, what's this Helen tells me about your little visit to the Legion yesterday?"

Wow. That Nan.

Darby felt lucky she didn't have to get past that kind of radar at home in Toronto. She'd never make it anywhere near the Eaton Centre with her skateboard, that's for sure.

As soon as the screen door slapped shut on the front porch, Darby raced into the little back room Nan called the scullery where she did the laundry. There was a big sink under the window and an old-fashioned washing machine with a huge basket of wet sheets on the top.

No dryer.

It took Darby about twenty minutes or so to hang up all the sheets on the clothesline behind the house. It was hot work, and she stopped for a minute in the middle to drink a huge glass of cold milk. When she headed back out to finish the job, she tripped over Maurice and almost dropped the last laundry basket. It could have been a disaster with all that red PEI dirt just waiting to get on Nan's white sheets, but luck stayed with her. Two minutes after pinching the last clothes-pin, she was rolling up to the end of the street in search of Gabriel.

On the way, Darby passed Red T-shirt kicking his soccer ball. Except that today, just to mess things up for her, he was wearing a green shirt. She waved at him anyway, ready to let bygones be bygones. But he was so focused on bouncing the ball off his knee, she ended up just cruising on by.

Proves my point, she thought. *Who's being unfriendly now?*

In the end, she didn't even have to look for Gabriel. She rolled up to the old blue house and flipped the skateboard into one hand. He was sitting right in front of the house, perched on the old rusty fence beside the gate.

"That doesn't look too comfortable," Darby said, with a grin.

He smiled. "I knew you'd come today. Everything is ready."

What kind of weird remark was that?

"Ready? Ready for what?"

He hopped off the fence and reached out a hand. "May I?"

Darby realized he wanted to see her skateboard. The truth was she had never let anyone lay a hand on the board before that moment. Not even Sarah. Then she thought about Red T-shirt ignoring her. And she *did* know where this kid lived . . .

"I guess so," she said, reluctantly. "But no riding it. I'm still breaking it in."

He nodded absently and turned over the skateboard in his hands, examining it carefully. He spun one of the wheels with a finger.

"Geez, you'd think you'd never seen a skateboard before," Darby said. "It's not a fancy one or anything. One day I'll get one with dual trucks."

He looked up at her as if from far away and handed the board back.

"I think it is beautiful," he said. He turned and started up the path to the house. "Are you coming?"

She shrugged and followed behind him slowly.

He paused to wait. "I see you have taken to wearing a moustache," he said, pointing at her upper lip.

Darby's cheeks reddened. She swiped a hand across her face. "It's nothing," she muttered, and repeated her earlier question. "What did you mean—all ready for me?"

He just smiled. "Have you had a chance to look around the town at all?"

Talk about avoiding the question. Darby marched through the long grass, following him around the side of the house. The little stone chapel and the crab apple trees behind it came into view. On this side of the house the paint was really peeling—hanging off in strips in places, with the grey, weathered boards showing clearly beneath.

"Gabe, you actually live here? Because I think your folks could use a little help with the upkeep."

He stopped a few paces ahead of her and turned to look up at the old house.

"I love this place," he said softly. "It has been in my family a long time."

Darby looked at him sceptically. He sounded sincere, but—

"Did you know my grandfather was born in this house?" she asked.

"Was he?" Gabe didn't look surprised.

"So Nan says. I guess in those days babies weren't always born in hospitals. But then something happened to his mother, and his father sold the house and moved away. I guess that's when your family bought it?"

He shifted his shoulders a little and bent to pick up something from the grass. The sun slipped behind a great grey cloud, rimming its edges with gold. The leaves on the giant oak tree at the very back of the property rustled and danced and the wind swirled the grass at Darby's feet, flattening it in spirals.

"You told me you thought this was just an old town filled with old people," Gabe said.

Darby stared up at the darkening cloud behind him. "Maybe it is," she said nervously. "What difference does that make to you?"

The wind whipped his hair around and the merriment drained out of his face.

"Perhaps I will show you something," he said.

"Well, okay—but can you make it quick? I'm no judge of the weather around here, but that looks like a serious storm cloud to me."

He didn't turn his head or even glance at the sky. Instead he held out his hand, palm up. Darby found it suddenly harder to see for some reason—maybe because the wind was whipping her hair into her eyes. She took a couple of steps closer. But it was only a rock in his hand. A plain, red, Island rock.

Something about the way he held his hand seemed strange, but Darby didn't take time to think about it. The wind had worked itself up to a roar.

"Look, Gabriel, this is going to be one huge storm," she said. "I need to get home. That's a nice rock and all, but we're just going to have to talk about it later. I've got to go."

Quick as thinking, his other hand shot out and grabbed her by the arm. "No time," he shouted over the wind. Or maybe he said, "Too far." Either way, she knew he was right. It was a couple of blocks to her grandparents' house.

As if to prove it, a sheet of rain swept down from the sky and she was soaked to the skin in an instant. Great. All the work hanging up Nan's laundry was wasted.

"Follow me." Gabe's voice somehow carried through the storm. There was a clap of thunder and something leapt straight out at Darby from the grass. She jumped, but it was only Maurice, her grandparents' cat, hanging out here again. He must have been looking for shelter because he hopped past them onto the stone windowsill of the chapel.

"This place doesn't look very safe," Darby yelled, looking at the half-collapsed roof and piles of rubble inside. Definitely more like a chicken-house than a chapel.

"Perhaps you are correct," Gabe replied. "But what choice have we? Please take my hand."

She grabbed on and they stepped up onto the windowsill. There was a blinding flash and the sky split in pieces divided by streaks so brilliant they left blue lines imprinted across Darby's vision. Unless they dashed across the entire expanse of back garden, the tiny stone building was their only hope for shelter from the storm. Darby didn't want to make the run, so she hoped it would be enough. She closed her eyes instinctively and clutched Gabe's hand as they stepped across the stone windowsill and inside.

The dark was absolute—and wrong. It took Darby a minute or two to figure out the wall of noise from the storm had stopped the instant they stepped inside. Just like someone had slammed a door on it. Darkness dropped around her like a smothering black hood. She couldn't feel Gabe's hand. She couldn't see any light.

The panic Darby felt rising with the onset of the storm threatened to erupt. She had thought things were bad when the darkness was on the other side of the bedroom door, but that had been nothing. Reaching for Gabe, she spun in a circle.

Nothing.

Waving her arms wildly, she tripped and fell, her head rebounding off the floor. It seemed to Darby that the darkness had taken not only her vision, but also her voice—or maybe she was just too scared to scream. One minute she had been yelling at Gabe over the noise of the storm, and the next . . .

Finally she just covered her eyes with her hands, wanting to make her own darkness and not have it pushed down on her against her will.

For some reason, it seemed to work. When she got up the courage to uncover her eyes, thin daylight outlined the stone frame of the window. The rain had stopped, too. Instead, mist rose up from the ground in a ghostly shimmer that was almost scarier than the storm itself. It slipped along the rock window and rolled over the sill like foam frothing over a waterfall. The already dim light of the outbuilding took on a grey tone she didn't like at all. And where was Gabriel, anyway?

"Uh, Gabe? I don't feel like playing hide and seek, okay?" she said, her voice sounding squeaky and scared to her own ears. She shifted a bit to one side and rolled up on her toes to see if visibility was any better higher up.

It wasn't.

Her stomach twisted into a knot. Trust your instincts, her mother always said. If a situation feels wrong, it probably is.

"Okay, this is just stupid." Stupid *and* embarrassing. Her voice sounded small and wavering, but at least she still had a voice.

Enough was enough. It was time to get scarce. "I'll be back tomorrow for my skateboard," she yelled into the misty room. "I'll be bringing my brother, and he's *really* big."

As soon as the words came out of her mouth, Darby cringed. An imaginary big brother? It had been a long time since she'd hauled him out. Must be a couple of years at least. One time she had run all the way home from school because some kids had stolen her bus pass. "My big brother will get you!" she'd yelled as she bolted onto Yonge Street. The kids just laughed. Probably the way Mr. Gabe the Mysterious was laughing now, wherever he was. "I'd better get that board back," she muttered to herself.

The mist had thickened so much she had to put her hands out to feel for the rocky surface of the window ledge. Bad enough to lose the skateboard. She didn't want the stormy evening to catch her in the creepy old building. Nan would never let her out alone again.

But something was wrong. More than wrong—weird. The stone windowsill had been right behind her. She had just hopped over it. She could still feel the spot where a sharp piece of rock had bitten into her palm as she climbed up onto it.

Darby reached an arm straight out to feel for the window. Nothing.

She shuffled her feet to one side about a foot. Still nothing. *The wall should be there. I should have bumped into it by now, or at least grazed my knuckles.* She shuffled sideways again.

"Oh, come *on*," she said aloud. First the storm and now the fog. What was with the weather in this place? But she'd freaked once and wasn't about to do it again. Still, the fog had her completely turned around. Stepping carefully so as not to trip again, she flung her arms out wide and slid her feet side to side. The only sound was her own breathing. Finally, when she felt ready to scream—her hand brushed something.

Not a rock windowsill. This surface was cold—so cold she yanked her hand away in surprise.

In the second or two it took to get up the nerve to reach out again, the temperature fell sharply. Darby's breath felt like ice crystals on her lips.

Ice crystals?

In summer?

What was happening? She took a panicky step forward and sure enough—she bumped her head. Hard. Hard enough to knock her to her knees. And as her knees hit the ground, they crunched.

Just as Darby figured out that the crunch was not breaking bones but rather the sound of frozen snow on the ground, she finally got what she had been waiting for. A light shone through the mist at last.

With the snow under her knees came a realization. She must have fallen asleep. There's no way this could be anything except a dream. The kind of dream where you find yourself in a place you've never been before and yet it seems somehow familiar.

That had to be the explanation. There she was, on her hands and knees in some kind of crunchy snow in the middle of the summer, wisps of fog swirling and fading all around. The only thing to do was to head for the beam of sunlight that gleamed like a beacon ahead. The sun grew brighter and the air was suddenly sparkling like prisms—pretty painful on the eyes, but Darby had never been so happy to see daylight in her life.

She crawled as fast as she could toward the source of the light. If there was a record for the fastest crawl through snow in cut-offs, Darby was determined to break it. The strangely glittering ceiling suddenly dropped, but after two head bumps in as many minutes, she just ducked down and beetled straight for the light.

By the time Darby got up the nerve to lift her head again, she realized she had crawled nearly twenty feet past the end of whatever weird tunnel she'd been in. And when she did look up, she wished she hadn't.

Around her was a world of white.

The sky was white. The ground was white. Darby had never seen so many shades of white; from blindingly bright, almost blue-white to a dull, flat white that pounded at her temples like visual static. Everything was white. Nothing was white. Everything was nothing; she couldn't identify a single object.

She staggered to her feet, one hand over the sore spot above her left eyebrow. First total darkness and then this? The whole dream scenario just wasn't making sense. This all-white world had to be a result of the knocks she'd given her skull over the past few minutes. Darby remembered the time she'd smacked her head on the curb when she'd first tried out the skateboard. That had been kind of like this. She rubbed the sore spot again. Okay, the truth was that nothing has ever really been like this, but the sense that her brain no longer quite belonged in her body was the closest feeling she'd ever had to this sensation.

That time, after the stars had cleared, her mother had plopped a helmet on her head and everything had been all right again, apart from a headache that lasted a day or two. But now there was no lecturing, helmet-bearing mother. There was no warm summer evening. Instead, there was cold. Deep, solid cold.

Darby had a sudden longing for one of Nan's geeky hand-knit sweaters. She touched her head again. It throbbed a bit but didn't feel so bad, really. She took a quick look at her fingers, too. No blood.

And yet everything was still white. She hugged herself tightly, tucked a hand under each arm and thought about the light. It had been a white light at the end of a tunnel. A chill penetrated her heart with the speed of a slicing icicle. Didn't people claim to see a white light just before they died?

She wiggled her eyebrows. Sure, there was no blood—on the outside. But what if all this was a hallucination brought on by bleeding in her brain?

"Am I dead?" she whispered, and then jumped a little at the sound of her own voice. She hadn't meant to speak aloud, but the fact she could had to mean she wasn't dead.

Didn't it?

"You're not dead, Darby."

The voice, so close to her ear, made her jump again. It was Gabe. Darby felt faint with relief. She spun around.

"Where are you?" she hissed, and then because she really wanted to know, "Where am I?"

"You'll see me soon enough. Just be patient, and watch for the helping hand."

What kind of answer was that? Darby made a mental note to find someone new to hang out with. Even Gramps was less weird than this guy.

"Gabe?"

No response.

She could have kicked herself for not listening more closely to the location of his voice. Maybe reasoning with him would work. Or bribery.

"Hey Gabe? Look, just take the skateboard if you want it."

Maybe that was a bad idea. She'd die for that skateboard.

On the other hand, she remembered the light and the tunnel.

"The board is yours, Gabe. Just get me out of here, wherever here is, okay?"

No response, but as though borne on the wind or from a long way off, she heard the unmistakable sound of his laugh. And at last a figure materialized out of the wall of white around her. A small figure in what looked like a brown hoodie walked toward Darby with an awkward, wide-legged stance.

Chapter Five

Adrenaline surged through Darby and she raced toward the figure. Almost right away she could see it wasn't Gabe. It was just some little kid, all wrapped up against the cold. All the same, she was so happy to see another human being, Darby thought the kid looked like an angel. As she moved closer, she could see so many layers of leather and fur on the small figure, she couldn't tell if it was a boy or a girl. Darby got within yelling distance, took a giant breath and then stopped dead. The dreamlike feeling came back in a big way. What if she couldn't talk—couldn't call for help?

Just then the kid looked straight at Darby for the first time. She could see little more than the eyes, but something about the walking style told her it was a little girl. The child raised a hand in greeting and Darby's heart lifted in her chest. Even though this child was so much smaller, she could at least lead Darby to someone who could help.

"I'm so glad you've found me. Where are we?" Darby babbled. The child didn't reply immediately but instead did something very odd. With one hand, she reached up and pulled away the soft fur scarf obscuring her face. She took two steps closer.

And sniffed.

Darby instinctively stepped back. *How weird was that?* But things quickly got worse.

She opened her mouth to speak again, but the child brushed past.

"*Atlée!*" the child called, and Darby spun on her heel in the snow, trying to grab the child's arm as she went past. "Mama!"

"Look, kid," Darby began, "I'm not your . . ."

A large group of people was standing immediately behind her.

Even after all that had happened in the last fifteen minutes or so, this was really disturbing. There must have been ten people there. How did ten people manage to sneak up on her like that? One of them stepped forward and the small child ran over to her.

The people were all Darby's size or even a bit shorter. Maybe a group of teens out playing in the snow? The one who stepped forward was talking to the little kid. Darby thought they must be babysitting or something, but if they had to take the little kid back home, they could take her, too. For the first time in as long as she could remember, she really wanted the company of an adult.

"I cannot see her, Mama Atlée. I looked

everywhere—I walked right to the breathing hole in the ice, but she is not there."

There was a low murmur of sound and several members of the group exchanged glances. The person the small child had spoken to bent down.

"You must not do that again, Sha'achi. Not even for Nukum. I know you are a big girl now, but it is not safe to go away from the family group all by yourself. If you travel alone on the ice, the *qallupilluq* will come along and steal you from our family. Do you want them to pull you under the water? Grandmama Nukum will be back soon."

Darby tried to shake off the strange feeling of dread that had settled into her stomach. Why hadn't the little child said anything about her? Even if the kid's grandma was missing, surely a shivering girl in cut-offs standing with snow up to her skinny white knees would warrant some kind of comment.

Darby stepped forward.

"What is the bad smell, Atlée?" asked Sha'achi. She pulled the fur off her face and sniffed the air again. "It smells like the breath of the bears. Are the bears here, mama?"

Darby shook her head in amazement. She'd been the subject of a few serious insults in her time, but no one had ever said she smelled like a bear.

But she was anxious and desperate enough to swallow her pride. She took another step forward in the snow. "Um, excuse me. Could one of you help me? I have no idea where I am . . ."

The person talking to the child stood up and pulled back her hood. Without the shelter of the encircling fur, her eyes creased against the brilliant light of the sun. "I do not know what the smell is, but it is not bears, little one," she said, not responding to Darby at all. "Come back inside and take some food. You must eat before we journey."

The group encircled the small child protectively and moved away from Darby. She closed her eyes in despair. This was too much. She'd asked for help and they'd just ignored her? The whole situation was so bizarre, all she could do was follow her only hope for information. She scurried after them, trying to place each step in the footprints they left behind in the snow.

In a moment, they began to disappear from sight and Darby wondered once again if she was seeing things. Then she realized they were dropping, one by one, into a low tunnel that led into the snow.

Her tunnel!

Darby picked up speed, slipping a little in the deep footprints, when she noticed that one person was standing apart from the others and had turned back to face her. The figure was slightly taller than the rest.

She slowed her pace as the last of the others disappeared into the black mouth of the tunnel. Her eyes had better adjusted to the light, and she could now see how the snow banked behind the tunnel. The person standing to one side raised a hand and pulled off his hood—for Darby could now see he was male.

He wore a carved bone tied with some kind of leather strip across his eyes for protection from the sun. As he pulled the bone away, she gasped in shock.

It was Gabe.

Before she could say a word, he put a hand up to his lips and gestured for her to be quiet. She found she had no words to say at that moment, anyway. He reached out and took her cold hand into his mittened one.

"I know you have questions, Darby, but time is very short. Just know that all is as it should be and while I am beside you, you are safe."

"But," she said, finding her voice at last, "why won't they help me? Why don't you? I want to go home."

He squeezed her hand. "You nearly *are* home, Darby. And they would help you with their very lives if they could. But you are not of their world and they do not really know you are here."

Darby shook her head in despair. This made no sense at all.

"What on earth does that mean—*not really?* They either know I am here or they don't. Which is it?" she peered closely into his face. It was such a relief to have someone to speak to—to touch. "Is this some kind of dream, Gabe?"

"This time is for listening, Darby, and for watching. I know it all must seem strange, but you will learn and next time will be easier. Now take heed."

He pointed with one arm and shouted. "*Nukum!*"

Immediately a rumble of voices came from the

tunnel, and several of the people spilled back out onto the snow. Gabriel pulled his hood up and slipped on his eye covering. He joined several other members of the group as they hurriedly strapped snowshoes to their feet, lashing them to their soft boots with leather laces.

Darby scanned the horizon, but apart from a small black dot in the distance, she could see nothing.

"Gabe!" She struggled through the snow to where he was standing. "What are you doing?"

She could just make out the flash of his smile inside the thick fur of his hood, but once again he ignored her and turned instead to the small child.

"Sha'achi, you must take your mother inside and get everything ready for Nukum. She will surely be very hungry and thirsty after her long journey."

He stood up, looked straight into Darby's eyes and inclined his head to indicate she was to go in the tunnel. Then he and a group of two or three others trudged off across the snow. The rest of the group slipped down into the dark hole.

But Darby remembered that tunnel. And the memories were not good. She did *not* want to go back in there, so she stayed right where she was.

Shading her eyes, she looked up. In a matter of those few moments, Gabe and his small party had travelled quite a distance across the sheet of snow. She was amazed at how quickly they could move on their snowshoes.

She was alone again.

Maybe it was the clear air, or more likely the pure rush of human contact, but Darby's panic began to roll back a bit. Her brain started thinking again.

Gabe's strange words danced through her head. "You are not of this time," he'd said. But how could that be? She patted her arms and gave herself a bit of a hug. She was definitely there. She was there and she was cold.

And yet not *that* cold. Not as cold as she should be. She was wearing regulation summer wear: an old yellow T-shirt of her mother's with a picture of Che Guevera on it, cut-off jean shorts and flip-flops. Correction: one flip-flop. She must have lost the other one in her scramble out of the tunnel.

The whole interaction since she had emerged into the blindingly white day had taken maybe ten or fifteen minutes. If she had been standing outside her Toronto house in December for this long, she'd have hypothermia by now. Sure, she was cold. But it was goosebump–quality cold, not freezing-to-death–quality.

But maybe a person couldn't freeze to death when they were already dead.

What other explanation could there be? The whole dream scenario didn't stand up—she'd just had a conversation with Gabe. Not a logical conversation, but they had talked all the same. And there had been that tunnel with the white light . . .

Yet, somehow, she just didn't feel dead. Of course, she didn't really have a basis for comparison. But her arms were covered in goose bumps and the spot over her eyebrow where she'd cracked her head the second time was very tender to the touch. And she couldn't even begin to list all the ways this place was different from any sort of afterlife she had pictured.

Darby looked down at her bare foot. Her toes were cold, but not freezing. In fact, the foot with the sandal felt just as cold as the foot standing in the snow. Gazing down, she noticed something else. Neither of her feet left marks in the snow. She was standing in a spot near the mouth of the tunnel where the snow was packed down by footprints, so she tried a little experiment. She took a step over to one side into a nearby snowdrift.

Big mistake. The snow had frozen and was crusty on the surface, but as soon as she put her whole weight onto the drift, she sank in right up to her thighs. She flailed around in panic for a few minutes before managing to drag herself back up onto the packed surface. In a moment she was back on her feet, hands on her knees and gasping for breath. Strangely, the effort to get free had actually warmed her up a little.

Once she had caught her breath, Darby glanced over to see if she'd actually made a snow angel with all her thrashing about.

There was no mark in the snow.

No sign of even a footprint, let alone evidence of a 110-pound girl flailing around for five minutes.

Maybe dead people can't make snow angels.

Carefully staying on the packed area of snow, Darby started pacing. *I should have listened to Gabe. If I*

went down in the tunnel, maybe I could get back home.
But the mouth of the tunnel was so black in contrast to
everything around it that she just couldn't make herself
do it. It was too much like crawling into her own grave.

Suddenly, Darby heard a shout. Gabe and his
group! She looked up to see them hurrying back across
the snowy plain, followed some distance behind by a
bounding yellowish dog.

They hadn't taken ten more steps when Darby
realized that the animal was as much a dog as she was
a chicken.

"BEAR!!!" she screamed, jumping up and down
and pointing. Gabe and one of the other group members were supporting a tiny person, no bigger than
Sha'achi. How they were moving so fast, Darby had
no idea. But they were not moving as fast as the bear.

Thinking about it afterwards, she was pretty sure
it wasn't a full-grown polar bear. She'd looked them
up in the encyclopaedia and knew they could grow to
be eight feet tall on their hind legs. The one chasing
Gabe and his group was not eight feet tall, but he was
plenty big enough. He had kind of a bumbly running
style, and at one point he actually stopped chasing the
group and rolled for a minute in the snow, like he was
playing. Gabe and the people with him didn't stop to
watch, though. They were pretty close now, and she
could see the strain on their faces as they tried to
make it back to the tunnel ahead of the bear.

As they staggered up, Gabe and one other guy in
the group half-pushed, half-carried the tiny person

toward the entrance to the tunnel. Darby turned to see
Sha'achi's little face framed in the opening. "*Nukum!*"
she squealed.

"*Nanuq*," corrected the old lady, for Darby could
now see that this must be the missing grandmother.
"Inside!" she commanded, and Sha'achi's face disappeared as the others thrust Nukum into the black
tunnel and scrambled in after her.

And in what had to be the strangest moment of
Darby's entire life, she turned to find herself face to
face with a polar bear.

Darby had done her share of school reports on
Canada's mammals. In grade five she did a huge proj-
ect on the Kodiak, a very large type of grizzly bear
found in the North. She distinctly recalled writing in
her report that Kodiak bears were the biggest bears in
Canada, even bigger than polar bears.

Standing on his hind legs, this guy was the
biggest thing she'd ever seen. Seconds before, she had
been terrified of plunging back into the black tunnel,
but it was amazing how the close-set eyes of a polar
bear gazing at her changed her mind.

The bear bounded up to the spot where the
snow was flattened and suddenly stopped. With
careful steps and a rolling gait, he moved toward the
tunnel, shaking his massive head back and forth as
he walked. Down on all fours, she noticed he was a
little pigeon-toed, but the size of his paws soon
drove anything resembling a clear thought out of
her mind. They looked as big as frying pans, with

claws as big as—well, as big as any claws she had ever seen.

He paused to one side of the tunnel, with his body directly between the snowdrift where Darby was standing and the tunnel. He put one front paw on the roof of the snow structure. In a moment he was towering over her, standing on his back paws and full out leaning on the top of the snow house behind the tunnel. The fur on his belly was pure white, or at least a little less yellow than the rest of him against the white ice of the snow house. She could actually see where his skin was almost black under the thick layer of fur, a black that seemed to emerge only with his sharp nose and again within his tiny eyes.

At that point she thought he might roar, or rip the top off the house and devour the inhabitants like a giant frozen people-pot pie, or turn and swallow her whole. But he did none of these things. Instead, he looked around in a nearsighted manner and, with his mouth open, noisily sniffed the air.

Darby stood frozen to the spot. Was it possible the bear hadn't seen her? A creature this size had to have an awesome sense of smell. If he hadn't seen her, then surely he could smell her now. It would only be a matter of seconds before she became a nice light snack.

He did see Darby. Saw her and smelled her. She knew he did, because he swivelled his head around and looked right into her face. He closed his mouth and made a kind of sing-song noise, half groan, half greeting. And then he tucked one shoulder under and rolled over into the snow, kicking his legs joyfully in the air like a dog asking for a belly rub. He rolled again, this time onto his feet, and lumbered around to the back of the snow house.

Suddenly, the power of movement returned, and before she could think about it twice, Darby dove into the tunnel.

—⟁—

The darkness she feared did not really materialize, because once Darby regained her feet she found herself crab-walking beneath the low ceiling toward a flickering light. Not a bright, beaming light this time, but two dancing flames, each contained within a small lamp. The smell from the lamps was very strong and her eyes watered with it. As she scrabbled into the room she could see there was a celebration of some sort underway.

Though most of the people had removed their outer clothing, Darby still felt cold. In fact, the inside of the little house didn't seem any warmer than the outside. All around her was much laughter and conversation—and not a glance was sent in her direction. She sidled along one wall to where Gabe sat off to the side, a little apart from the celebration.

There was a lot of happy noise, so she risked whispering to him.

"Can you talk to me now? Can you please tell me what is going on here?"

He inclined his head slightly, and barely moving his lips, said: "Words must wait, I'm afraid. Things will be clearer with time. For now you must sit and listen and when the time comes, watch for the helping hand."

He turned away then and joined in a conversation with the man beside him. No amount of tugging on his shirt made him pay the least attention to her.

It was the second time he had mentioned the helping hand. What was he talking about? But she was too discombobulated to be angry with him, so in the end she crawled across the fur rug that covered part of the floor, sat leaning against a wall and did as he said. She listened.

Sometimes taking advice can actually pay off. Once Darby settled with her still-cold hands tucked underneath her armpits, she began to learn a few things.

The smell from the lamps faded out as she listened. The people she had thought were teenagers all turned out to be, with the exception of Sha'achi, adults. Their faces showed their age, and the grandmother's face was the oldest of all, wrinkled like a rusty apple. They were all strongly built and certainly not very tall, though it was harder to tell in the small interior of the snow house. The house itself was surprisingly spacious, with the floor and walls made of firmly packed snow, and fur rugs and mats scattered around for everyone to sit on. There was no fire or fireplace. The only heat seemed to come from the lamps and the bodies of the people, and everyone seemed warm enough, except Darby. The same cold lingered on.

The good news was that Darby had found her missing flip-flop, tucked right inside the tunnel entranceway. The bad news was that it warmed her up not at all. She thought again about the knobbly sweater that Nan had knit for her last Christmas, and just the thought of it made her eyes well up with tears. Would she ever see Nan and her strange knitting experiments again? Darby made a vow that if she did somehow make it out of here, she would try to be more patient and kind to Gramps. She would be the model granddaughter. If only she knew how to get home.

"Nanuq has brought us good fortune," said one man, in a voice louder than the rest. The other voices in the room quieted, and Darby could see that it was the man sitting beside Gabriel who was speaking. His voice was low and warm, and he spoke slowly, as though his words were very important.

"We have come through a time of great loss," he said. "For the people this has meant much hunger and many long journeys. But the coming of Nanuq means the coming of joy."

"Is it spring, Mushum?" squeaked Sha'achi, and everyone laughed.

"Yes, granddaughter, Nanuq's visit means spring is not far away. And the fat seal we will eat tonight is yet another sign."

Nukum's thin voice rose above her husband's. "In my journey, I have seen the most important sign of all—the *atikuat* are near."

"You are right, grandmother," came another voice. Darby jumped a little when she heard Gabe speak. She realized that he was speaking in the language of these people.

He was speaking and Darby was listening—and understanding.

This thought actually made her head spin again. She rested her face down on her knees for a few minutes while she tried to get used to the idea. She didn't even know the name of this language; how could she understand it?

After a few moments the sick feeling passed, and Darby tried her best not to think about it again. Gabe had said everything would be clearer with time, and she had no choice but to take him at his word. When she lifted her head again, he was still speaking.

"And so we must follow the caribou, as we have ever done, even though it means new territory for the people. Because for the people, *atik* means life."

Nukum leaned forward. "When I left on my journey, I carried with me a heavy load," she said. "My heart was heavy with fear, but my arms were also heavy. Along with the fear, I carried hope, in the form of stones to mark our passage. Now that I have seen the *atik*, it is important we remember *all* of the people. We must use the rest of the stones we carry, together with those we find on our path, to mark the way so that the other families will find their way to the *atikuat* as we have done."

There was a general rumble of agreement to this, over which Mushum's voice could be heard.

"Before we begin this last journey to our spring hunt, we must celebrate the visit of Nanuq. Let us feast!"

With his words, Darby could see the dull flash of metal above his head. He plunged a knife down into the carcass of a seal that was lying on some kind of sheet of tanned leather in front of him. Thankfully, she hadn't noticed the seal before this moment and she tried to quell the surge in her stomach as he cut up and distributed the meat. The blood of the animal was carefully drained and most of it set aside in bags made of skin, but some of it was joyously shared as well. It was obvious how important this feast was, and Darby suspected the people in the snow house hadn't eaten very well lately from the enthusiasm with which they enjoyed their meal.

Conversation carried on long after the food was gone, and Darby's head nodded. Voices travelled through the air and it was hard to follow exactly who was speaking.

"This hunger has chased us far too long. We must make changes."

"We have always followed the herds. It is the spirit of the caribou that has changed. The spirit wanders far. We must follow."

Darby was still cold. She listened to talk of where the journey would take the people, of new landforms not seen before and perhaps even different animals to add to the hunt.

"We must mark the way," one voice said.

Darby thought about the distance the people would have to travel to find the caribou. She thought some more about the bear and whether it was just waiting outside to gobble her up. And finally, she thought of nothing, because leaning against the ice wall of the cave, sleep came and stole her away before she even knew she was gone.

Darby didn't know what awoke her. Can the sound of quiet act like an alarm clock? Whatever it was, she suddenly sat up with a start, having keeled over onto the icy floor sometime in the night. It was not quite pitch dark, as a little grey daylight crept through the passageway. There was enough light for her to see that everything filling the place last night was gone—the fur rugs, the flickering lamps and what scared her the most: the people. Including Gabe.

How could she have slept through everyone leaving? How could she have slept at all? Darby racked her brains frantically. In a best-case situation, this was a dream, and she couldn't recall ever sleeping *inside* a dream before.

Her heart started to pound, but then she realized

she'd never heard of anyone sleeping and then waking up again through their own death, either. Anyway, she didn't have time to freak out. She had to put her dark side on hold, stifle her fears and go find Gabe. He was her only link to normal, and Darby was determined not to lose him again.

The next step was to get up the courage to once again climb out through the tunnel. Though she no longer feared the white light at the end, the polar bear was something else. It was only the thought of how much her delay was costing in terms of finding Gabe that finally pushed Darby through the doorway.

To her vast relief, there was no sign of the bear when she climbed cautiously out through the passageway. But there was no sign of Gabe or the people, either. And how would she ever find them, especially wearing flip-flops?

In the end, Darby used the tried and true method of walking in their footsteps. There was no other choice, really, and luckily it hadn't snowed since they had left. The small amount of daylight was already fading and she hurried on, head down except for the moments she took a quick peek to ensure Nanuq hadn't changed his mind about a Darby appetizer.

She tried not to think about the oddness of the situation, but she couldn't help worrying about the cold. And she had another little problem. Her stomach was seriously starting to rumble. Darby had no idea how long she had been in this strange place, but she did know she needed to get herself some food, and soon.

Even the raw seal from the night before was starting to look pretty good in her imagination.

The thought that Gabe may have dropped something on the trail she might be able to eat made her look up, so in the end she credited her stomach for getting her out of the biggest jam of her life. Because that's when she saw it.

Not a snack left by Gabe, but rather Nukum's helping hand. Darby couldn't believe Nukum had left it there for her, but help her it did. She had been struggling up a low hill for some time, and now in front of her, on a spot where the wind had swept the snow from the rocks, she found it. Nukum and her family had done as she had promised and left a sign for the people who were yet to come. Over the crest of the hill in the last pink light of the day, she could see far below the tiny group of people as they worked together to make another shelter, this one of rocks and skins, for the night. Beyond them, a herd of caribou as huge and widespread as her eyes could take in was grazing on the first shoots of greenery on a vast, windswept plain.

And beside Darby? She rested her hand on a low pile of rocks—a stone marker, pointing the way to the future for The People yet to come.

Chapter Six

Something wet and cold was running down Darby's cheek. She reached up to rub her fingers through it. Was it blood? Her head was pounding so hard she could hardly open her eyes, but when she checked, there was no blood on her fingers. She tried to sit up, but a wave of nausea hit her and she decided to stay put for another minute. This was no ordinary headache. Even with her eyes closed she could see spots dancing like— like snowflakes.

That got her up. As she lifted her head, the headache slammed home like an axe through her skull. But she had to think. She had to think.

Snowflakes. What had happened to the snow? She squeezed her eyes open a crack, but all she could see was grass. Grass with yellow flowers dotted here and there.

Darby was in the secret garden. Her skateboard was on the ground and she sat with one hand on the stone windowsill of the old building.

She wiped her face again and realized that what she

had thought was blood was actually saliva. She must have been lying in the garden, drooling on herself.

Disgusting.

Darby tried to scramble to her feet, but her stomach heaved and pretty soon the drool wasn't the only disgusting thing she left in the garden.

She couldn't ever remember a headache like this one. With wincing eyes, she glanced at the stone windowsill. Had she fallen and hit her head? It was so hard to think.

The sky was clear, with a few wispy clouds turning pink at the edges. No sign of a storm at all. Darby could see a single evening star gleaming through the leaves of the huge oak tree. The light of it pierced her brain and forced her to look away. Under her feet, the grass was a little wet, but it felt more like dew than the remains of a cloudburst. Hadn't it been pouring when she was last here? Darby had to put the thought aside—she needed all her energy just to get herself up off the ground.

There was a rustle and Maurice jumped out through the window and down onto the grass beside Darby. He meowed and circled around her feet, a calico figure eight.

"Better watch where you're stepping, cat," she muttered to him and he purred at the sound of her voice. The spots seemed to be fading and the headache had eased a little since she had been sick, but she knew she had to get back to Nan and Gramps. Maybe she'd given herself a concussion. Her head was so sore she didn't even want to think about what she had just been through. How long had she been gone? Had the police been looking for her?

Darby felt a weird pang of guilt. Poor Nan. She must be out of her mind with worry. But it was so hard to think with her head pounding. She wished with all her heart to be home in Toronto, but she also knew Nan would know what to do. Nan had brought up Darby's dad and his brothers, and being the mother to three boys meant she had probably seen enough cracked skulls to know what one looked like. Darby just had to get to her, first.

As she stood up, Maurice leaped through the garden toward the front of the house. By the time Darby had staggered around there, she could see him zipping through the rusted gate and heading for home. She followed, moving pretty slowly. Every step jarred her head and the red late-afternoon light was making her feel nauseated again.

Nan met her at the door. "Have you been chasing Maurice, Darby? He's all worked up," Nan began, but her words died on her lips when she got a look at Darby's face. "What's the matter, dear?"

Darby dropped her board on the front porch with a clatter that made her wince. Not one word about how she had been gone for two days. Nan was just upset about the cat? A pain was stabbing through the back of Darby's right eye and she couldn't think anymore. She muttered something about hitting her head and before she knew it, Nan had her wrapped in a comforter on the couch in the living room with a cold cloth over her eyes.

And once again—she was gone.

Darby woke up sometime later to find Nan standing beside her spot on the couch with a strange man. Before she had a chance to say a word, Nan explained he was a doctor who lived across the street. The guy was wearing shorts and an apron splashed with barbecue sauce. Nan must have pulled him away from his dinner.

She stayed in her spot on the couch and listened to them talking beside the door.

"Are you sure she's going to be all right, Brian?" Nan said, her voice worried.

The screen door creaked on its hinges. "I really don't think you have any cause for concern, Etta," he said, in what Darby recognized as the reassuring tone doctors always use. "There is no sign of physical trauma. She's at the right age for getting a migraine—teenage hormones often play a big part. Migraines are terrible things, but they don't cause any lasting damage and they are more common than you might think. Just bring her along to my office tomorrow when she's feeling better and we'll do a couple of standard tests."

The door slapped behind him, but only after Nan pushed a home-made apple pie into his hands.

Darby couldn't imagine her own mother ever giving a doctor an apple pie. Darby wasn't even sure her mom knew how to bake. But then again, she'd never heard of a doctor who would do a house call in Toronto, especially wearing an apron that said "Kiss the Cook."

After he left, Nan helped Darby upstairs to her room. Darby was surprised to find Gramps sitting on her bed. He waited until she was finished in the bathroom and had her pyjamas on, and then he tucked her in and kissed her on the forehead.

"Goodnight, kiddo. Sleep well." That was it. He left and Darby heard him walking down the stairs, talking to Nan.

It felt weird—but in a nice way. And at least he hadn't called her Allie.

—⁓—

The next morning, the first thing Darby saw was her school journal sitting on the table beside her bed. Her clock said it was only 6:30. No need to go downstairs just yet. When she sat up, she found her head wasn't hurting at all anymore. In fact, she felt pretty good. She grabbed the journal, intending to write just a line or two to eliminate any feeling of homework guilt she might have—not that she had much. She started to write what she could remember about the people in the snow house. It might have been a hallucination, but it was pretty interesting all the same.

Her memory seemed a little clearer now that her head had stopped aching, too. She remembered that long walk in the snow, climbing the hill and seeing the huge herd of caribou in the distance. She remembered touching the pile of boulders on the crest of the hill, and seeing how the rocks formed a sort of stone figure with two squat legs. And she remembered—

Darby rolled out of bed to find the denim shorts she had been wearing yesterday. After much tossing of clothing from her drawers, she checked her laundry basket and sure enough, there they were.

She jammed her hand into the pocket and pulled it out. In her palm sat a fragment of green stone. Darby ran her thumb over the surface. It had a strange texture to it, almost soft.

Her memory told her she had picked up the stone from the base of the larger pile of stones. But if that was all a hallucination, how could it be lying in the palm of her hand?

And what about Gabe's rock? The one he gave her before the storm hit—the big rainstorm that should have ruined all of Nan's white laundry. Nan hadn't said a word about it, but then, she'd been worried because of her granddaughter's headache.

Darby remembered they'd been about to take shelter from the storm and Gabe had held out a rock. A piece of red sandstone, just like the green one Darby now held in her hand. He never told her what the rock was for, or why he held it out in the first place. She couldn't even remember putting it in her pocket. But when she reached back in the pocket, there it was.

And what about Gabriel? Mr. Mystery himself. Just a few days ago, Darby had thought Gabe might be the one kid in this weird little town she could actually talk to. But now she was not so sure.

Darby lay back on the bed and put the rocks beside her on the pillowcase with the notebook. The few lines she had meant to write had turned into ten pages filled with wild scribbling. Rocks and strange friends and polar bears. Not that she would ever show it to anybody. She's not *that* crazy. But it had felt good to write it down.

The strangest thing about the whole experience was the passage of time. Darby had been—well, wherever she was—for at least one night. She *slept* there, for Pete's sake. But the date on her watch had not changed. Could she have bashed the watch? It *seemed* to be running just fine, the seconds ticking away . . .

The next thing Darby knew, it was eight o'clock and Nan was knocking gently on the door, asking if she might care for a little breakfast.

When Darby called out a sleepy good morning, Nan's worried face appeared around the corner of the door. "Are you feeling any better, dear?"

"I'm fine, Nan. I guess it was just a migraine like that doctor said."

She tucked the rocks and her journal into a drawer. "And actually, I'm pretty hungry."

Nan opened the door wider and beamed at her granddaughter. Nan's hair was sticking straight up and she looked like she hadn't slept that much herself, but the relief on her face was obvious.

"I've made pancakes for your breakfast, dear," she whispered conspiratorially as they walked down the stairs. "Gramps might act a little out of sorts to miss his porridge, but I think the bacon may win him over."

As it turned out, Gramps was talking on the telephone when they entered the kitchen. He ruffled Darby's hair a little as she walked past him and then waved her to a spot at the table. She sat down and got started on the pancakes before he had a chance to protest.

"Nothing to worry about, Allan. She's fine this morning. She's sitting at the table eating your mother's pancakes right now. I know, I know—but one day without porridge won't kill her."

This was a shocker. Gramps was talking to her dad? Darby couldn't remember her dad ever talking to Gramps on the phone. Nan, yes, but . . .

Gramps winked at Darby. "Now, here's Etta."

There is no explaining old people.

Gramps sat down and tucked into his plate of pancakes and bacon. He didn't even make a crack about the amount of syrup Darby was eating. Nan talked to Darby's dad a while, adding her reassurances and even saying her granddaughter was good company to have around.

Who knew?

Nan shooed Darby away from the dishes, so she went out to the front step. Her stomach was full of pancakes and bacon and her skateboard was calling, but she had some serious thinking to do.

Darby leaned back against the screen door and closed her eyes. She had never heard of migraine headaches bringing on visions. And yet the hallucination about the people in the cold was so vivid. She could still feel the snow crunching underfoot. How could people live like that? *Did* people really live like that?

She opened her eyes. Not a snow house in sight. But if she wanted answers, she knew where to find the next best thing. No hope of Googling—no such thing as a computer under *this* roof. Instead, she hopped inside to ask permission and picked up her favourite means of transportation. Without a computer, there was only one place she might be able to get a few answers. The library.

Nan had no chores planned for Darby because of the headache and seemed very pleased when Darby said she was heading to the library. "Just remember your doctor's appointment this afternoon," Nan said. "And if you pick up any books of poetry, you might want to bring them back to read in that little park across the street."

"Uh—I don't really read much poetry, Nan," Darby mumbled, as she slipped out front door.

"That's where I met her, y'know," said Gramps. His voice startled Darby—she hadn't known he was on the porch. He sat at the small table with an old scrapbook open in front of him.

"Not really in the park, y'see, because there wasn't a park there in those days. Just the old graveyard. Yer mother had a notion in her head that reading poetry in the graveyard was a romantic endeavour."

"Not my mother. You mean *Nan*," Darby said, but his eyes were distant and she wasn't sure he'd heard.

"Yer brothers used to play there, too. Tanned the hide of that young Al when he knocked over one of the old grave markers. An imp, that 'un. Paddled his behind more than once."

He mumbled a little more, but Darby snuck out the door. There was no way he had been talking to her. For one thing, she didn't have any brothers. She paused on the second step, the image of his face still in her mind—eyes distant—even a little lost. Darby sighed. This was one complicated visit.

She hopped on her skateboard and sped down to the library and spent a full hour looking up the history of northern Canada. Darby hadn't been to the public library in Toronto in at least the past year, and here she was in the Charlottetown library twice in one week.

Unheard of.

It was more than a little scary how real that hallucination had seemed, but Darby decided she must have subconsciously known most of the facts from work she had studied at school. Maybe in grade four or five? She seemed to remember a unit on the Inuit, but she didn't remember learning a lot.

The row of computers along the wall were all busy, so Darby turned to a staff member. When she asked for help finding information about the earliest people who came to Canada, the woman laughed.

"Oh, I'm not teasing you, dear," she said kindly, in response to the look on Darby's face. "It's just that before the European explorers came to North America, we don't have a written record of the history of the people who lived here. It's considered prehistory, actually."

She rummaged around and found Darby a book on the Beothuk, a very old culture that had been wiped out by diseases the explorers brought with them. She also handed Darby a book written by some professor who had a theory that the way the first native people came to North America was over a land bridge on the Bering Strait.

"It's a bit of a tough read," said the librarian, "but basically, he believes that the first nations people came to North America more than twelve thousand years ago across a frozen land bridge in the very northern part of Canada. This was before anybody was writing things down, mind you, so I'm not sure we will ever know the truth."

"It says here they followed the herds of caribou," Darby said slowly, reading the book jacket. "Can they tell from fossils, maybe?"

That sent the librarian off in yet another direction. By the end of the hour Darby had enough books to read for a year. She glanced over as someone stepped away from a computer on the end—she figured a few sheets of information from Google would have been a lot lighter to carry home. But the librarian had done so much work; Darby sat down to leaf through a few volumes in the big stack.

It was weird, though, because as Darby turned the pages, a lot of what she saw seemed strangely familiar. She read how the pile of stones the people left behind to show the way they had travelled was called an *inuksuk*. The book said *inuksuit* might have also been used to show nomadic people the way when they were travelling through the north. And an *inuksuk* has even been used as a modern-day symbol for the Olympic games.

After reading for an hour, Darby started to feel a bit sick, so she closed the books and piled them all on the cart. Her head wasn't really aching like before, but she still couldn't make sense out of her experience and it made her stomach upset. There was no denying she'd had a migraine. Even thinking about it made her stomach turn a little, remembering how bad it was. But could a migraine make her feel like she was being chased by a polar bear, or imagine she was sitting in an ice-house with people from another age and culture?

As Darby walked out of the library, she caught sight of Shawnie's poster inside a display case. Along with the poster were some samples of her work, but Darby's eyes were drawn like magnets to a tiny stone bowl sitting beside a little basket and some other small woven pieces. Darby dropped to her knees and peered into the case. The bowl looked so familiar—where had she seen it before? Maybe it would be a good idea to take Nan next door for tea, after all.

Darby had hoped that talking to the doctor would give her more answers, but when she asked him about seeing things during a migraine, he talked about spots and distorted vision. She could feel her impatience rising—nothing he said shed any real light on what she had been through. She asked if bumping her head would have given her a concussion, but apparently she didn't show any of the signs. The doctor smiled at her and said the road to adulthood is a rocky one. He added he was sure Darby had suffered from a common migraine. She rubbed her temple, remembering the sensation like an axe chopping through her skull. Nothing common about that feeling—at least not for Darby.

If he'd been wading through the snow with me, I bet he wouldn't be so quick to blame the experience on a so-called common migraine, she thought.

After the appointment, Darby skated back home and dug out the helmet her mom had packed for her. Whether the doctor believed it was a concussion or not, she didn't ever want to have a headache like that one again.

Darby spent the next few days poring over her library books and making notes in her journal. When she slowed down enough to check, she realized she had generated enough material to write an entire essay on the people of the North. But she still didn't know what any of this had to do with her. And on top of that, she hadn't been on her skateboard since she'd come back from the doctor's office. She piled the books on Nan's table by the door and grabbed her board.

Hanging out in the sunshine practising ollies off the curb made her feel a whole lot better. After an hour, she had figured out the foot placement, pushing down as hard and fast as she could on the back end and dragging the board into the air with her feet as she leapt up. She still couldn't get the board to flip in the air, but it felt good to have made so much progress.

Yesterday's experience seemed so fresh when Darby was reading about life in the North; but outside, gliding along in the summer sun, polar bears and northern people seemed a lot further away.

After another hour, she headed in the front door for some of Nan's lemonade. Gramps was still sitting on the porch with his scrapbooks. Darby stopped to look at one as she bent to put away her skateboard, and a picture caught her eye. It looked like it had been cut out of a newspaper: a group of young men all in uniform. She'd seen a few of Gramps's scrapbooks around the house and they all seemed to relate to his time in the war, so this was no surprise. But someone had drawn on this picture. Circles and crosses. The page almost looked like a tic-tac-toe game.

Darby leaned over his shoulder and peered at the picture. "Who's that, Gramps?" she asked, pointing at the face of one young man who was heavily crossed out. "I can't see his face with the x on it."

She regretted saying anything as soon as the words were out of her mouth, because she could feel Gramps's shoulders stiffen. But when he spoke his voice was soft.

"This is my old unit, kiddo. I seem to remember this picture being taken shipside in the harbour, before we set off for Korea."

"But why have you drawn on everyone's faces? How can you tell who is who?"

He shrugged and didn't answer right away.

"I never forget a face, kiddo. Some came home and some didn't. I don't need a goddamned picture to remind me. I remember every face in that unit."

Afterwards, Darby realized she probably should have left it at that. In the back of her mind, she could tell he was starting to get upset, but the picture really had caught her interest and she was curious.

"Okay," she said, leaning across the table, "who is that guy, then?" Darby pointed to a man in the second row whose face was heavily crossed off. "Or that guy?"

Suddenly, Gramps pushed his chair from the table

with such explosive force that his scrapbooks went flying, scattering all over the porch floor. His chair toppled behind him and Darby was so startled she jumped back with a squeak, narrowly avoiding having her toes crunched by the falling chair.

Gramps was standing looking at her, his eyes blazing in a face that had paled to the colour of sour cream.

"How dare you?" he said, his voice low and dangerous. "How dare ye touch the faces of those men?"

His voice started to rise now, and spit was flying from his mouth as he spoke. "Those men are my brothers. Harry Johnson lives on Cameron Street. His face is gone. His FACE IS GONE!"

Gramps's own face had changed colour from sheet white to brilliant red in the space of a single sentence. Darby had no idea what to do. She just wanted to get away. But she was stuck in one corner of the porch with the table that Gramps had pushed aside jammed into her legs.

"Gramps," she began, but he was past listening.

"Who are ye to speak about these men?" he roared. "Who are you? Identify yourself IMMEDIATELY!"

Darby's mouth had gone completely dry. She tried to say something but couldn't get any words to come out. She feared the old man was going to burst a blood vessel, or kill her, or both, when Nan stepped into the porch. She stepped right in front of Gramps and placed one hand on each side of his face.

He looked at her in fury for a moment, and then without a word he suddenly curled into her arms, sobbing like a baby. She rubbed his back while he cried and shot Darby a sympathetic glance over his shaking shoulders.

Darby closed her mouth and swallowed convulsively. In under a minute the day had suddenly darkened in spite of the late-afternoon sun outside. Gramps's sobs tapered off and she managed to quietly work her way out from behind the table. She put her hand on the screen door and Nan gave her an apologetic little smile.

"Time for tea, Vern," she said to Gramps as she steered him into the house. "I need you to open the new box of oatcakes ..."

The rest of her words were lost to Darby as she fled out the front door.

She was half a block down the street before she realized she'd left her skateboard on the porch.

Darby sank down to sit on the curb. What was going on with Gramps? She'd heard of old people losing their marbles, but this was so weird and awful. Her stomach felt like a mass of snakes were coiling and squeezing inside and she wished she were at home, far away from the old man. *Now I know why Dad never came back here,* she thought.

A door slammed behind her, and with her twitchy nerves on edge, she jumped right to her feet. She had been sitting in front of one of the houses that was built almost right up against the street. No front lawn—just a screened-in porch and stairs. It was cranberry red with blue and grey trim around the porch and gables, and the breeze was rustling a fat bed of tiger lilies against the sidewalk. A woman stood on the steps by the front porch.

"Sorry," Darby blurted.

The woman grinned broadly at Darby. "For what, may I ask?"

Darby didn't know what to say. Sorry for sitting on a public street in front of your house? Sorry for having such a weird grandfather? Her mouth opened to speak but nothing came out. In the end, the woman took pity on her and laughed.

"Don't be silly. You can sit there any time you like." She stepped down off the porch. "You're Darby, aren't you? Vern and Etta's new granddaughter?"

It was Darby's turn to laugh a little. "Not exactly new," she said. It felt so good to be talking to someone normal that she started babbling. "I mean, I'm thirteen, so I've been around for a long time. But I've only been here a week and a half, even though it seems like longer. I really live in Toronto, and I'm just visiting while my parents are renovating our house."

The woman nodded, still smiling a little. She looked like she was somewhere in her early twenties. She wore her long hair in two loose braids and she tucked a flyaway strand behind one ear as she spoke. "Renovating, eh? That's a bummer. But you get to spend time on the Island for the summer, so that's a bonus. And your grandparents are such great people."

Man, did she have that wrong. But before Darby could straighten her out she spoke again.

"Speaking of renovations, I've been meaning to drop by ever since you got here, but I've been so busy at work. I've got something I think you might like."

Darby felt baffled. Something for her?

The woman walked down her steps and heaved the large, black leather bag she'd been carrying into the passenger side of her car. It was a little Smart Car, bright red, so it almost matched her house. There was really only room inside for the bag and the woman. Darby closed the car door for her automatically.

"Thanks, Darby." She grinned again. "Good Gaelic name you've got there. I'll drop by after dinner tonight. See you then!"

She hopped in the front seat of her car and drove off.

Darby leaned against the splintery wood of the hydro pole and watched her go. She'd been so busy spilling her own life story that she'd forgotten to ask the woman's name. There had been a UPEI parking sticker in the back window of her car. Maybe she was a student at the university. Darby resolved to ask Nan about the woman later on—when she got the courage to go back to the house.

Somehow, talking with Smart Car lady had made Darby feel a bit better. The sick feeling was gone from her stomach, at least. But she was outside and her skateboard was still in the house, and she didn't feel like facing up to crazy Gramps just yet.

Darby glanced up the street toward the old blue house, but she wasn't about to go poking around there yet, either. Just seeing the house reminded her of the killer headache.

She wandered back to Nan and Gramps's house and sat on the front step, trying to get the courage up to go in to say sorry to Gramps. Darby didn't think she had done anything really wrong, but she didn't mean to upset him like that. And she *was* sorry.

The screen door squeaked a little and Darby jumped to her feet, but it was only Nan. She had a large glass of lemonade in one hand and a small glass of some kind of copper-coloured liquid in the other.

"Oh, girlie, I'm so sorry," she said. Nan's voice sounded like she'd been crying and that made Darby want to cry, too.

Instead, Darby tried to cough the lump out of her throat. "Is Gramps okay?"

"Sit down, my dear, and have a sip of lemonade" she said. "I'm so glad you're here. After what Dr. Brian told me, I was worried the scene with Gramps might bring on another one of your headaches."

They sat down and Nan had a big drink out of her glass, which made *her* cough a little, too. "Sherry," she said, by way of explanation. "Lemonade just isn't enough for your old nan at a time like this."

"I'm really sorry I upset Gramps, Nan," Darby said in a low voice.

"Oh, darling girl, you didn't upset him." This was odd, but instead of saying anything else, she had another sip of sherry.

"I made him spill his scrapbooks all over the floor," Darby said. "He seemed pretty upset to me."

Nan set her glass carefully down on the step and took one of Darby's hands.

"I just meant that *you* didn't upset him, Darby," she

said. "Your dad may have said something to you about this, but your Gramps has always had a bit of a temper."

Darby shook her head. "Dad never talks about Gramps, Nan. Mostly he just talks about work."

She sighed. "I guess that doesn't really surprise me. Your dad and your grandfather are more alike than either of them will ever admit, and they've had their share of bumping heads over the years. I've always felt your grandfather's temper was the reason that your dad never brought you to visit us, dear."

"He's never really said anything about it," Darby answered, doubtfully. Her dad didn't really say too much about anything, but he never had a bad temper, either, at least that she'd noticed. But maybe that was why Dad never seemed to talk to Gramps on the phone.

"Well, whatever happened in the past, I am very happy to have you with us now, dear," Nan said.

"Gramps isn't," Darby said, and all her worry came blurting out in a rush. "I should never have mentioned the picture. It's just, well, I've never really talked to Gramps about his time in the war and he seems to think about it a lot. But I came from him and from you, and my dad never talked about Gramps, either, really. I mean, I knew Gramps had been in the war, but I didn't know anything about it. I guess I just thought he might like to tell me some of the details. I didn't mean to make him mad."

Nan shook her head and squeezed Darby's hand. "I haven't even told your father about this, but after that shameful display today, you are entitled to know. Your grandfather is not just some bad-tempered old man, and you deserve to be treated better than the way things worked out today."

She sighed again, and her face suddenly looked very old. "I've been watching Gramps for the past year or so—he's not been himself for quite a while. When he and I went to the doctor's appointment last week, Brian—Dr. Brian—well, he confirmed a very big worry I have had about your grandfather for some time."

"Is Gramps sick, Nan?"

"Yes, dear, in a manner of speaking, he is. Brian told us that Gramps might have a condition called Alzheimer's disease."

Darby had heard that term before. She didn't really know what it meant, just that it was something that happened when an old person's brain stopped working right. Poor Gramps. Poor Nan.

She hugged her grandmother hard. "Does that mean he has to go into the hospital, Nan?"

"No, at least not yet. I've told Dr. Brian that I can manage Gramps just fine at home. After the incident in the tree the day you arrived, Brian wanted me to have Gramps admitted to hospital. But he has been so normal since then . . ." She put her face into her hands for a moment.

Darby felt terrible. The last thing her sweet old Nan needed when she was dealing with such a scary thing, was to have some rotten granddaughter around, messing up her life.

"I should go home to Toronto, don't you think, Nan? Wouldn't that be easier for you?"

Nan raised her head and actually smiled a little before draining her glass. "The doctor said a glass of sherry every day is medicinal, under the circumstances," she said, and patted Darby's hand. "Actually, my dear, it was your presence that convinced Brian to let Vernon stay home. Having your sharp eyes around is such a help. That and the fact that he lives just across the street, himself."

She stood up. "Time for me to make dinner, darling girl. We can talk about this more another time. Let's just keep it between ourselves at present, shall we?"

Darby nodded. What else could she do?

"I promise I won't be responsible for putting a terrible strain on you," Nan continued. "I hope what happened with Gramps today was an uncommon situation. Brian did say that we should expect some unusual behaviour. For the most part, Gramps is just a little forgetful. And as long as he stays that way, you and I will manage just fine. But if things get worse or he has another episode of anger like today, I want you to know I'm ready to talk to Brian about some of our other choices."

Darby followed her into the house. "If he's feeling better after supper, I'll do the dishes with Gramps, okay Nan? And I can help peel the potatoes, too."

Nan squeezed her in a little hug. "Peeling the spuds before dinner and doing the dishes after? What more could an old granny ask for?"

How about a husband who isn't losing his mind? Darby thought. But she didn't say it. She just smiled at Nan and closed the door.

Chapter Seven

That night, Gramps seemed completely normal—no sign of any anger or concern toward Darby at all. She said sorry for spilling his scrapbooks, but he acted like nothing had happened and even offered to go through them with her sometime.

How can a person forget a huge blow-up like that? Darby sat at the kitchen table after finishing the dishes and tried to think of a good reason. It seemed so weird; it was almost seemed like there were two of him. Gramps bright and Gramps dark. She smiled a little. Maybe she wasn't the only one in the family with a dark side, after all.

After dinner there was a knock on the front door. Nan scurried to open it and Darby could hear the surprise in her voice. "Fiona! What brings you here, my dear?"

Nan walked back into the dining room, followed by the woman from the cranberry-coloured house down the street. She was staggering under the weight of a pile of big boxes, so Darby jumped up from the kitchen table to help her.

"Fiona, this is my granddaughter, Darby," said Nan. "And Darby, this is Fiona Grady, our neighbour from two doors down."

"We've met already, Mrs. Christopher," said Fiona, propping the boxes between her hip and the wall. "I've been meaning to bring these things over for Darby, but I forgot until I saw her today."

She smiled as Darby lifted the top box off the pile. "You know, after I met you earlier, I realized that we are cousins, in a way."

This was news.

"Here, let me help you." Nan bustled over to take another of the smaller boxes from Fiona's pile. "You know," she said, "you are quite right about that, dear. Of course, we didn't really work it out until your grandmother passed on, did we?"

"That's true," said Fiona. She turned to Darby. "I think one of my great aunts was a cousin to one of your great grandmas, or something like that," she said. "Big Irish family. I can't keep them all straight, to tell you the truth."

"It's the Scots that keep things organized," said Gramps, and he thumped the wall beneath a tartan plaque hanging above his chair.

"I didn't think Christopher was a Scottish name," said Fiona.

"My mother made the mistake of marrying an Englishman," he barked. "But before that, it was all highland Scots. My mother was a MacLeod and her father was from the Urquharts out of Inverness." He pushed his chair away from the table. "What have you got there, young lady?"

Fiona grinned a little at Darby before answering him. "Well, Mr. Chris, I know you haven't had any kids in this house recently, so I figured this one might need a little in the way of, uh, *contemporary* fun," she said. "I didn't really have a chance to talk much to you today, Darby, but you should know that I review software for a living. When my grandma died, I inherited her house, so I work at the university part time and the rest of the time I play games on my Xbox at home."

"Wow! Dream job," Darby said, impressed.

"Yeah, it can be pretty cool," she said. "But it also means that I have a bunch of old hardware lying around, so I thought you might get some use out of it."

Nan and Gramps with a PlayStation in their upstairs bedroom? Darby couldn't believe her ears.

But Fiona meant every word. She had brought over an old TV, too, and she and Gramps and Darby wrestled the boxes up the back stairs and set it all up on the desk in Darby's room. Gramps complained the whole time that children today were far too spoiled for their own good. Once the equipment was in place upstairs, though, he patted Fiona on the back.

"Guess this means I won't have to fight over the remote with the kid anymore, right?"

Oh, right. Like I'd ever get a shot at the remote with him around, Darby thought. But she was too happy—and too smart—to say it out loud.

He hurried down the stairs to catch the end of some

movie called *Pork Chop Hill,* and Fiona and Darby got to work on the hookup.

"There's no chance your grandparents have an Internet connection," Fiona muttered after Gramps had stumped off down the stairs, "but even though you can't go online, this should save you from total boredom on a rainy afternoon."

Darby couldn't thank her enough. "This is *so* cool," she said, checking out the game packages in one of the boxes. "I can't believe you'd do this for me!"

Fiona sat down on the bed and rubbed her back a little. "Hey, I spent a lot of time with my grandmother when I was growing up," she said. "Her family had come here from Ireland a long time ago, and let's just say it's not only Scottish people who have a thrifty streak." She grinned. "I grew up loving computers, but whenever I visited Grandma, there would be none of that nonsense. She'd send me outside to play, which in retrospect was probably a good thing."

Fiona got up to stretch and leaned out the window. "Look at that! You can see the side of my house from here."

She pulled her head back in. "Anyway, when I heard you were coming to stay, I thought about all the stuff I have hanging around my place. And it can't hurt to let you have just a little connection with the modern world now and then."

"Thank you so much," Darby repeated, as they walked down the stairs. "There hasn't been much to do around here, apart from skateboarding. And Gramps doesn't really like the noise my skateboard makes, so I can only practise farther down the street. I've been hanging out with a kid named Gabe, but he's, uh—"

Darby didn't know what to say about Gabe and didn't really want to go there, anyway. "He's only around once in a while, so this will be great!"

"Oh, yeah?" Fiona said. "Is he the kid with the soccer ball?"

Darby shook her head. "No, that's some other kid. Gabe lives in the blue house at the end of the street."

Fiona looked at her sharply. "The *blue* house? I didn't think anyone was living there right now."

Darby shrugged. "Nan says an American family has bought it to use as a summer house, but Gabe's family speaks French, so I don't think it's the same people."

"Hmm. Maybe his people are renting it before the construction crew comes in."

"Construction crew?"

"Yeah. I met the American family last summer," she said. "They showed me the plans for the new house. It's a beautiful design. It will fit right in on the street and nobody will know it's not 150 years old. But it's going to be all wired up inside. A smart house."

"Kinda like your Smart Car?"

Fiona laughed. "Kinda." She put her hand on the doorframe and called through to the kitchen.

"Thanks for letting me share my stuff with Darby, Mr. and Mrs. Chris!"

Nan appeared from the kitchen holding a large plastic container of cookies. "No, thank *you*, dear," she said in a loud voice. She thrust the cookies into Fiona's hand and whispered, "Mr. Christopher is a little old-fashioned, dear. Just ignore his grumbles. It was lovely of you to think of Darby, we do appreciate it."

"Not at all, Mrs. Chris," said Fiona, and the moths buzzed around her head as she stepped out of the shelter of the screened porch into the evening air. "If I'd known there would be cookies involved, I would have been over much sooner!"

Darby waved goodbye and bid her grandparents an early goodnight. She'd spied the package for a skate-boarding game that looked wicked, so she bolted up the back stairs and spent a happy three hours making virtual ollies and kick-flips off superhuman-sized ramps.

Later, when she stopped to think about it, those were three hours well spent. Because in the end, it was the only time Darby used Fiona's gift for the rest of the summer.

———ᗡᗡ———

The next morning Darby awoke with sore wrists from playing with a game controller for the first time in so long. Now that things seemed a bit calmer with Gran and Gramps, she decided it was high time to find Gabe and sort through what had really happened after they had walked through that window.

To be safe, Darby washed *and* dried the breakfast dishes for Nan, and said she'd be back to help some more before lunch.

But Nan had other plans.

"I have a little surprise for you, dear," she said, rummaging in her purse.

Darby hated hearing those words from parental-type units. Their idea of a little surprise didn't usually translate into her idea of fun.

Nan waved a pair of tickets that she had dug out of the deep recesses of her purse. "Shawnie Stevens popped over yesterday while you were out and brought me these," she said cheerily. "She has a special opening of her art show with her husband, Michael, today. When she was so generous to bring over the tickets, I offered to take her to coffee, and she agreed."

Looked like finding Gabe was going to have to wait. Darby started to worry a little when Nan asked her to wear a dress to the art show, but luckily since she hadn't actually brought a dress with her, they settled on a nice pair of shorts and the hideous sweater Nan had knit Darby last Christmas.

It was a beautiful morning, clear and hot without even a hint of breeze. As soon as they stepped outdoors, Darby's hair stuck to her forehead, but she kept the sweater on anyway. Gold star for the good granddaughter.

Shawnie's art show was on display in a little gallery on Grafton Street near the downtown mall. Darby and Nan arrived just after the doors opened, and only a few people were milling around. Shawnie was at the back of the gallery, but when she saw them she waved and came up.

"Mrs. Christopher! Thank you so much for coming."

"Darby was thrilled to get the tickets this morning, Shawnie," Nan said, staring at her granddaughter pointedly. "I couldn't keep her away!"

"Yes, thank you for inviting us," Darby said, in her gold star voice. She knew a cue when she heard one. Especially when delivered by Nan.

"Let me show you around a little," said Shawnie.

"Oh, we wouldn't dream of tying you up on your first day," said Nan. "We'll just have a quick peek around ourselves."

Darby had to give a few mental gold stars back to Nan for that one, saving them the pain of the guided tour. And anyway, she wanted a closer look at the little piece she had seen in the display case at the library.

Almost right away, Darby got lucky. Nan made a beeline over to chat with a friend she spotted, so Darby was free to wander around and try to find the little stone object.

Looking at the artwork, Darby decided the poster Shawnie had put together didn't really do her own work justice. For one thing, the pictures were all of her husband Michael's work. Half of the room was taken up with the artwork he'd done. There was a picture and biography of him on the wall, and she recognized him a few minutes later talking to Shawnie. He worked with porcupine quills and sweetgrass, weaving detailed designs on baskets of different sizes and shapes.

When Darby looked at the table set up next to the baskets, she caught her breath. Shawnie's stonework. The stone had etchings of old symbols, and the little text description said they were called petroglyphs. But mixed in with the petroglyphs were a number of figures carved out of stone. The one that caught Darby's attention was carved in the shape of a walrus. She picked it up. It was very heavy in her hand but the stone was soft.

Soft and green.

She had a piece of stone that looked just like it sitting on the desk in her room. And her mind flashed to the soft stone lamp in the people's dark snow house. Shawnie's initials were carved in the bottom of this walrus, and Darby glanced in her direction. Her mind swirled with questions.

Just then, someone put a hand on Darby's arm. Nan looked a little startled when Darby screeched, then tried to cover it with a cough.

"My goodness, dear, I'm sorry to startle you. Shawnie has agreed to a five-minute tea break," whispered Nan. "Perhaps a little warm tea will help that cough of yours, as well."

Good idea. Darby grinned and followed the two women to a little tea shop farther down Grafton Street, turning over the carved walrus in her mind.

At their small table, Nan set down two cups of tea and Darby chose a glass of chocolate milk. Nan put milk and sugar in her tea and Darby offered Shawnie the small pitcher.

"I didn't grow up drinking milk," she said with a laugh. "No matter how hard I try, I just can't get a taste for it. I'm lactose intolerant, so that makes it even harder."

Darby hardly gave Shawnie a chance to stir her tea before she started firing questions. "How come you carve things like seals and walruses out of rock? I didn't know there were walruses in PEI."

She laughed. "No—you're quite right. I haven't seen any walruses around lately. I'm not from here, though; I was born in Rankin Inlet, so I carve the animals I grew up with."

"Oh, I thought you were a Mi'kmaq," Darby said. "I didn't know you were from the Arctic."

"My husband, Michael, is Mi'kmaq. He is a member of the Abegweit First Nation and he grew up just outside of Charlottetown in a little place called Scotchfort. But I didn't grow up here. We met when we were going to art school in Toronto, and after we got married we moved here to be close to his family."

"So is your family still in the North?" Darby asked, trying her best not to let Shawnie see she was holding her breath.

"Yes, they are mostly still in Rankin Inlet. My family are Inuit."

Ha. I knew it. Darby felt strangely as though a puzzle piece had just snapped into place.

"Um, so, I'm kind of interested in the stone you carve," she said. "It's not much like the stone around here or even the rocks we have where I live in Toronto."

Shawnie looked over at Nan. "You have a very clever granddaughter here, Etta." Nan beamed, and Darby briefly had visions of getting out of doing dishes for at least a week.

But Shawnie was still talking. "The rock I use for carving is called soapstone. It's found mostly in the North. When I work with it, it reminds me of home. I also like to carve on bone, and sometimes I use clay to make sculpture, as well."

"Michael carves his images into rock too, doesn't he?" asked Nan. So she had been doing more than chatting with her friend at the show, after all.

Shawnie nodded. "Yes. We both like to produce artwork that reflects our cultural heritage. It was fun going to school in the south, though, and not just because I met Michael there. It was fantastic to see the work of other Canadian artists, and I think they have had an influence on my work as well."

She told them she had gone to the Ontario College of Art, and Darby spent a few minutes filling her in about some of her favourite places in downtown Toronto. Turns out they both missed being there.

Funny.

After Shawnie went back to her show, Nan and Darby wandered along University Avenue before heading home. As they walked in the front door, Nan handed Darby the plastic bag she had been carrying.

"Here's a little something for you, my dear, just as a remembrance of your stay with us."

Darby opened the bag and inside was one of Michael's baskets with the image of a starfish woven into the lid.

"Thank you, Nan. It's beautiful," Darby said. And it was.

"Oh, it's not very practical, I know, but I'm glad you like it all the same."

"I do like it, very much," Darby said.

She was surprised to see Nan's eyes fill with tears. She leaned across and gave Darby a short, sharp little hug and then shook her head.

"Enough of this foolishness," she said. "Darby, I brought up three lovely boys into grown men, but I have no experience with having a teenage girl around. Thank you for coming with me today. You have no idea what a difference you have made to our lives this summer."

And then, because she was Nan, she went straight into the kitchen and cleaned it within an inch of its life.

Darby walked upstairs slowly, and put the pieces of red sandstone and green soapstone into her new basket. She suddenly had a lot to think about.

—m—

After lunch, Darby grabbed her board and set off down the street. Forsyth Street wasn't a long one, but as she cruised along, she had to admit it was more interesting than she had first thought. Some of the houses did look like cracker boxes, it was true, but at least they were different from one another. At home, Darby's friend Caitlyn Morris lived quite far up Yonge Street, two towns away from Darby's place, in Richmond Hill. Where Caitlyn lived, the builder decided that originality was an old-fashioned idea. Her house looked exactly the same as the houses on either side, right down to the same tree planted in the same spot out front.

None of that could be seen where Darby stood on Forsyth Street. On one corner was the little store where she ran to get milk for Nan and red licorice for herself, if Gramps was in the mood to spot her the cash. Across from it was an empty house with a For Sale sign in the window. Beside that house was Nan and Gramps's place, with its big tree in the front and its crisp white front porch. And Shawnie's bright yellow house was next door. On the other side of Shawnie was Fiona's cranberry-coloured house.

They definitely went for bright house colours in Charlottetown. But somehow they hadn't seemed so colourful when Darby first arrived. The street itself was tucked in beside Prince Street, and was so small it didn't even appear on any of the maps of Charlottetown she had seen.

Darby pumped her foot again. Across from Fiona's house was the old park, and now that she was looking for it, she could see the tiny little graveyard that Nan and Gramps had been talking about the other day. She pulled up on her skateboard for a minute, propped it against a tree in the park and checked her watch. Only 2:30. Plenty of time for a quick look.

The graveyard was behind a church that faced the next street over. Darby's first thought as she walked through the grass was that it had to be the least scary graveyard she'd ever been in. The grass had grown tall and lush and there were flowers everywhere.

Walking through the grass, her toe caught on something and she went sprawling. It was a gravestone, sunk to just above ground level. After Darby recovered from bashing her knee in the fall, she brushed a few branches and leaves away from the top of the stone.

The inscription was almost worn off, but she could see a name. It said:

Annie (or could it be *Hanna?*) *Rourke Grady, b. 1828, and her infant daughter, Mary. Died 1849.* Underneath, it said *Dreaming of Home.*

Dreaming of home? What did that mean? Darby had never seen an inscription like that. Not that she made a habit of wandering through graveyards. She thought headstones usually said *Rest in Peace* or *A Loving Mother* or something like that.

Strange.

She was on her hands and knees, trying to read the inscription on another headstone in the shape of a cross, when someone cleared his throat behind her.

She turned to see Gabe leaning against one of the few large stones that hadn't actually fallen over yet.

"I did not want to startle you," he said.

As if.

"Why? Do I look like the nervous type?"

He crinkled his eyes at Darby and pointed. "See that Celtic cross? This is an old Catholic cemetery. I do not think anyone has been buried here for more than one hundred years."

"Hmm. So my Nan told me. She used to read poetry here when she was a girl."

Gabe stepped away from the stone. "Truly? It seems an odd place for reading."

Darby looked around. "I thought so too, but now I'm not so sure. I mean, there is nothing remotely scary about this place. It really is sort of peaceful." She looked at him. "Kinda like the garden at the back of your house."

He grinned. "When it is not in the middle of a storm,

perhaps." He trudged toward Darby through the knee-high grass. "There are a lot of peaceful places around here," he added. "The Island is very pastoral."

"Pastoral," Darby snorted. "Whatever that means. If it means quiet, it sure didn't feel very pastoral last week."

"Truly?" Gabe said, his face all innocence. "I did not notice."

"And where have you been since then, I'd like to know?" Darby demanded. "That was the freakiest experience of my life and you just disappeared. Some friend."

"I was there when you needed me," he said in a low voice, and turned on his heel toward the park.

Darby hurried along after him. "I needed you when I came back out through the window," she said. "I had the worst headache of my life. I didn't see you anywhere."

"Ah." He raised his eyebrows. "I have heard that can happen."

Darby picked up her skateboard and put her other hand on his arm. "Just what *did* happen back there?"

He shrugged. "You tell me."

This was infuriating. She opened her mouth to yell at him when she realized she had trailed along behind him all the way to the end of the street. They were standing outside his rusty front gate.

"When you arrived here, you seemed very unhappy. I remember you said this place was awful, not like your home. The people were all old and not interesting. All you wanted was to get away. This is true?"

"Okay, yes, maybe I did say that," Darby admitted. "But that still doesn't explain what happened in your backyard."

"What happened is that perhaps you learned something about the *dull* people who live here. And maybe you even got away for a little while, hmm?"

Darby laughed. "The people in that hallucination, or whatever it was, didn't live here, you idiot. They lived in the North. There was a *polar bear,* if you recall. Not exactly what I'd call dull." She suddenly realized that if it was a hallucination or the product of a bumped head, then there was no possible way Gabe could know about the polar bear. And yet he didn't seem confused by her lunatic ranting in the least.

"Whatever you say." He paused for a moment. "My question to you is do you have enough interest to learn more?"

Enough interest? *Enough interest?* Gabe had been around for less than fifteen minutes and he was already making Darby nuts. Why wouldn't he tell her what she needed to know?

"There is no way I am going through that window again," she said. "You have *got* to be crazy."

"Perhaps," he said, smiling like a loon. "Or perhaps I just want to help open your mind a little."

"*Opening your mind a little* is learning how to knit on Friday afternoons," Darby snapped at him. "Or taking a philosophy class in summer school. I think this qualifies as just a little more serious than that."

He turned and walked toward the back of the house.

She ran after him. "Where are you going? I just said I wouldn't go through the window again."

"I heard you," he said. "I am just going to inspect it

to see if the storm left any further damage." He turned to look over his shoulder at her while he was walking. "I wouldn't want any loose stones to fall onto your head."

"There was no storm," Darby yelled, following him in spite of herself. "There was no storm and there was no polar bear and I just had a very bad migraine headache!"

By this time she was yelling so loudly her throat actually hurt, but Gabe just stood by the big oak tree, acting as if everything was normal.

Everything wasn't normal.

There was no cloud or sign of a storm in the sky, but the air still felt charged somehow. The hair on Darby's arms stood straight up.

Just as she was about to turn on her heel and run home, Maurice came slinking from beneath the big hedge that separated the yard from the back lane. He was stalking something. A bug, maybe? But somehow, she couldn't take her eyes off him. He looked like a small tiger with his black, orange and white patches, creeping along, totally focused on whatever it was he was chasing. And he was getting closer to the old chapel.

All of a sudden, he launched himself forward like a coiled spring and with a loud yowl he snatched something out of the grass.

It was a rat. A huge grey rat that was half as big as Maurice. It was not dead, but still struggling, whipping its head back and forth, trying to bite Maurice with its giant yellow rat teeth.

Maurice sprang to the stone windowsill, and with a single shake as he jumped, he broke the rat's neck. Then he turned his head in that weird way cats have to proudly display his prize to Gabe, and launched himself off the stone windowsill into the old building.

"That was totally disgusting," Darby said, turning to look at Gabe. "Are there more rats like that around? Because if there are, I am so out of here . . ."

But Gabe was no longer standing by the tree. Instead, he'd stepped up onto the windowsill himself, as if checking out where the cat had gone with his dead rat prize.

"What are you doing?" she whispered.

Even though she knew.

He reached up and ran his fingers along the stones of the windowsill. "No loose rocks here," he said, and held out his hand.

She stared at his hand and felt the air hum.

"I will stay by your side," he said softly.

She couldn't help herself. Her stomach clenched— with excitement or fear or . . . she didn't know what.

"I have to be back to help Nan with supper," she said, stepping up beside him. Her mouth had gone totally dry.

"You'll be back," he said, and she felt his warm hand around her cold fingers as they stepped through the window together.

Chapter Eight

There may not have been a sign of any storm, but the crazy fog was back. It rolled up over their feet before Darby and Gabriel had even stepped across the windowsill and jumped to the floor below.

By some miracle, Darby made a perfect landing on both feet, into what turned out to be a big puddle of fog-shrouded water. Gabe splashed down beside her and she had one glimpse of his water-spattered grin before the fog swallowed him up.

"Remember," he began, his voice still right beside her ear, but then he was gone.

"Remember what?" she bellowed into the fog, but the mist swirled and circled and filled her mouth and eyes and ears with a roar that sounded like wind and water and smelled like salt.

At least it wasn't dark. It wasn't dark, but it was wet. Wet and cold. A cold Darby recognized. It wrapped around her like a blanket, but without any warmth or comfort. She took a step forward and felt her feet splash again, and then the floor tipped straight sideways and she flew through the air with a yell.

She found herself jammed into a corner with a pile of loose rope and bits of rusted iron and netting. Light shone in from around a small hole in the wooden wall through which a rope was dangling. It was also through this hole that much of the water appeared to be flowing. The only difference Darby could see between the wide planks of the floor and the wall was that the wall was more splintery. But only a bit. Her feet were flung over her head in a position her gym teacher would probably have said was good for her flexibility. But at the time, it mostly hurt.

She didn't really have time to endure the pain, though, as the floor tipped again, this time the other way. Darby managed to turn herself right way up, but she still slid along, tangled in nets and feeling every splinter from the rough floorboards on her bare shins. A rope hanging loose from the rafters slapped her in the face and she grabbed it and clung on.

This turned out to be a good kind of accident, because when Darby looked up, she could see the rope hung from some kind of cleat in the low wooden ceiling. It meant she could plant her feet and hold on without slipping too much as the floor pitched from side to side.

Why was the floor pitching, anyway? And why was she alone, dangling from the rope, in some closed-up wooden room that looked nothing like the little broken-down chapel behind the old blue house? She didn't have a clue. What she did know was that, once again, Gabe had disappeared.

Darby wasn't sure how long she spent dangling and pitching, but it was long enough to leave her arms very tired. It was also long enough to figure out a few things, only one of which was really important for the moment.

This was *no* hallucination. She knew pain when she felt it, and her right shin really hurt. And while Darby had her share of crazy dreams in her life, this was not one of them. She clung to the rope and counted the reasons out loud.

"One: Dreams don't have splinters." The floor pitched sideways again and water washed up over her shoes.

"Two: Shoes do not get soaked in dreams." Well, unless you counted that unfortunate time when she was four and mistook her mother's closet for the bathroom in the middle of the night. But hey, she was a little kid.

The floor seemed to be settling down, so she risked letting go with one hand to give her shoulder a bit of a rest on that side. Luckily, Darby had been riding the subway since she was small, so her shoulders and arms were almost used to his kind of abuse. She had just switched sides when the door flew open with a crash of iron and a splash of more water. Darby jumped and let go of the rope entirely, retreating until she could feel a solid wall at her back.

A man with black eyes that looked ready to pop out of his brilliant red face bodily flung another fairly small man onto the floor right at her feet.

"Ye'll stay in 'ere until I can bear to lay eyes on you again, ye filthy Mick bastard," he spat.

The smaller man at Darby's feet just curled in a ball, and a good thing, too, as he was given several angry kicks by Bulging Eyes.

She flattened herself against the wall and waited for the anger to fall upon her next, but neither man took any notice.

"The next time ye steal from the food stores, ye bloody thievin' wretch, it'll be the fishes 'oo gets fed. Not that there's much meat on those pestilential bones o' yers." With a last kick—one that actually missed— Bulging Eyes stomped out of the room and slammed the door so hard Darby's ears rang. The sound of an iron bolt closing with a crash immediately followed.

She stood frozen to the spot. If the man at her feet wasn't dead, he must be close. But just as she bent over to check, he uncurled with a groan. Darby could see he had dirty black hair that might have been curly if it hadn't been so matted. Over it, he wore a soft, mashed-up hat that slipped off as he rolled onto his back. And she couldn't take her eyes off a trickle of blood that ran from the corner of his nose along the line of his jaw.

Before she had time to think, he opened his eyes and looked straight at her. "I'm not dead, in case that is your hope," he said.

The face was plenty dirty, but Darby would have recognized those blue eyes anywhere.

"Gabe!"

"The same," he said, rolling to one side with a wince.

Darby dropped to the floor. "You're hurt!"

"The brilliance of you this morning outshines the very sun," he said, and made it over onto his knees with another groan.

His voice sounded strange, but Darby didn't really take the time to think about it. She stuffed her hand into the pocket of her shorts and pulled out the tissue that Nan had given her earlier.

"It's clean, at least," she said, and reached over to wipe the blood away from his nose. "You look like somebody who lives in a garbage can."

He smiled and shook his head. "Thank you, but that will not help just now."

"Don't be so stubborn, Gabe," Darby said, and took another swipe at the blood on his face. This time he just sat still, gazing at her patiently. She couldn't get the blood to budge.

"That's so odd," she said slowly, looking from the clean tissue to the fresh, wet blood on his face.

Gabe reached up, grasped her wrist and gently pushed her hand away.

"I think we have a few moments," he said, and slid over to lean against a wall. "Now that we are out of the open ocean, the captain will be very busy for a while. Too busy to return to a problem thief in his brig for a few moments, if all goes well."

It was hard to take it all in, and Darby could make sense of only about one word in three. The one that stuck in her head for the moment was "ocean," but only because she had been hoping she was wrong.

Careful of the splintery floor, she slid herself back against the wall to sit beside Gabe. He took the opportunity to swipe at the blood on his face with one of his filthy sleeves, which only served to smear it. This did not add to his allure.

"Our time together is likely short," he said in a low voice. "And there are a few things you must know."

"How did we suddenly go from 'I'll stay by your side' to 'our time is likely to be short'? And why are you talking with that funny accent, anyway?"

He lifted a hand warningly. "Now, Darby Christopher, I know how much the sound of your own words pleases you, but just try to keep them inside your mouth a moment or two more."

"But I don't get any of this," she said. "I don't have a clue where to start."

"I know it to be true," he said softly. "And you can ask all you like, but there's only so much time for the answering."

This made no sense at all, but Darby reluctantly agreed. She'd listen first, and then it would be her turn. But she couldn't resist a single question.

"This is like the last time, isn't it? It's a different place, but the feeling is the same."

He nodded. "There is much you must know," he said insistently.

She hugged herself tightly and tucked her fingers under her arms. "It's the same cold that I remember," she said. "I'm so cold."

"I am sorry," he said. "For it is part of the price paid."

"Price? What are you talking about?"

He muttered something, but Darby couldn't hear him over the sound of voices. Voices outside the door, growing louder and angrier by the minute.

"I fear the captain returns," said Gabe, and he actually did look scared. "I knew our time together might not suffice. Listen carefully, Darby. You are not of this time, but that does not mean you are safe from its reaches. If you are lost here, then lost you will stay. You must . . ."

The door flew open and a giant stepped inside.

Okay, so maybe he's not an actual giant, thought Darby, *but he's one big guy.* The man was seven or eight inches more than six feet tall, and he looked even larger, slumped over in the low-ceilinged room. Tiny beady eyes that were too close together under a single black eyebrow gave him a Cyclops look. Behind the giant was Captain Bulging Eyes. His eyes were bugging out a little less than they had been earlier, but he had a nasty grin on his face that Darby didn't like the look of at all.

"'Ere 'e is, Alec. The one who's been stealing your dinner."

Alec didn't say a word. He just picked up Gabe by his collar and dangled him effortlessly, toes just above the plank floor. Gabe squeaked and the captain's grin broadened. "What shall we do wif' the nasty little thievin' boy from the bogs, Alec?"

Alec's expression didn't change. "Throw him over, Cap'n?" he said in a strangely nasal voice.

The captain strode across the room until he stood right in front of Darby. "My very thought, Alec. 'Ow clever of you to read my mind." He paused for a moment, and then sniffed the air. Darby backed up as tightly as she could to the wall.

The captain sneered at Gabe. "Ye smell like a woman, ye thievin' cur. 'Ave you stolen the scent from one of the poor wretches below, or perhaps just 'er purse?" He turned to the giant. "Shake the little rat, Alec, and see what comes of it."

Alec did what he was told and poor Gabe was joggled until his teeth rattled together. But nothing fell out of his pockets except a small wooden comb that he had clearly not been using recently.

Alec threw Gabe down on the floor in a heap.

"No purse, then. Yer luck is wif' ye this time, boy," said the captain. "But I don't trust ye as far as I can throw you. I'd put ye down below with the others if ye weren't one of the few still strong enough to stand. So it's here ye'll stay until I decide what to do wif' ye."

"I cannot stay strong for long with this rough handling and poor food," said Gabe as he rolled onto his knees.

The captain jerked his head and Alec slapped Gabe back down to the floor.

Darby gasped out loud. She couldn't help it. She'd never seen a grown-up hit a kid like that before. It was sickening.

"The food is for the crew, ye wee rat, and you are to get no more than is doled out," snarled the captain. "I need every one of me crew hale and strong to get out of this place." He slapped a hand against the open door. "No amount of coin is worth these losses."

He turned again to the giant. "Pick up that sorry mess, Alec. I've sails that need mending. He can work off the price of the food 'e stole."

Alec hauled Gabe up by one shoulder and headed for the door. Gabe caught his hand around the doorframe for a moment and looked straight back in at Darby.

"If I had no chains on me, I'd wander the ship and try to pick up some news," he said clearly.

The captain had stopped to wrap the bit of dangling rope Darby had been clinging to around some loose pieces of sacking that were stored above her head. A strange noise rumbled up from his chest. She realized he was laughing.

"Y' really are a madman," he said to Gabe. "Talking aloud to y'self are ye now?"

Gabe didn't take his eyes off Darby. "It is true, sometimes I talk to myself. Is this not something all folk do from time to time?" he said. "I'm only saying, that since I will be on the deck repairing sails for you, Mr. Captain, sir, I will not have the chance to wander free around to hear and see all that is happening on the ship, much as I would like to."

"Ah—I knew ye for an idiot the first time I laid eyes on ye," the captain growled. "Ye picked the wrong vessel to sneak aboard, and ye'll earn yer passage like the rest." Alec grabbed Gabriel firmly by one ear. And in case that wasn't enough, he twisted Gabe's arm behind his back until he winced, and then frog-marched him to the door.

The door slammed behind them so hard that it bounced open and didn't latch. Darby sank back down onto the floor and tried to gather her thoughts.

So.

Here she was again. Or more to the point—here she *wasn't*. She wasn't at home anymore. She wasn't in her own time and she wasn't even sure she was in her right mind.

But.

She also wasn't scared. Not really. For one thing, there was very little chance that a polar bear would be chasing her anytime soon. Just the thought of it brought a quiet laugh to her lips.

Darby had handled a lot this summer. She'd been yarded out of her regular life, dumped by her parents with a crazy grandfather, and found out that not everything she'd grown to believe was really what it seemed. The polar bear was the clincher, though.

She still didn't know if that thing had really been chasing her or if it was just a phantom product of one killer of a headache. But if Gabe wanted her to have an open mind, he could rest assured now—her mind was open. She was desperate to find out more.

It made her feel better that she was not alone. Gabe might not be right at her side, but at least she knew roughly where he could be found: on deck, mending sails under Alec's watchful eye, no doubt.

He had risked another smack on the head to tell Darby to get out of this strange little room, have a look around and learn something.

So that's what she did.

Chapter Nine

Darby put her eye to the crack of the open door. Peeking out, she discovered the room was at the foot of a short flight of stairs leading up to an open deck of the ship. No one was in sight, so she crept up the stairs and peered over the top.

It seemed a large ship. The biggest boat she had ever been on was the Wolfe Island ferry in Lake Ontario, and this one was bigger than that by far. However, it was not in very good shape. The decks were made out of rough timber, and like the little room below, no one had taken the trouble to sand off the splinters and rough spots. There was a huge, rusty pile of chain attached to an old anchor nearby and several heaps of wood scraps were strewn all over.

The place was a mess and it stank.

It was a strange combination of smells: dead fish, woodchips, and something else that reminded her of hydro poles. Creosote, maybe—or tar? A little fresh air would be nice.

Darby took a chance and climbed another step to get away from the smell and to gain a better view. From her new vantage point, it looked like she was at the back of the ship. Most of the action appeared to be happening up at the front, for the moment, so it was pretty quiet where she stood. She took a moment just to breathe in a big gulp of the air—so fresh after the stale stench of the little room below. The sky was blue and the sun was shining almost right above.

A gull flew over her head with a raucous cry. His shadow blocked the sun from Darby's face for a moment—and gave her another thought. She raised her hand over the brightest part of the deck.

No shadow.

This convinced Darby more than anything had so far. Even more than the polar bear. Because, after all, no one ever gets eaten by a polar bear while asleep. At the time, she had considered the possibility of being deep in a dream. But this was just too clear. She couldn't walk through walls. But she also didn't leave footprints in the snow or cast a shadow in the brightest of sunlight.

Something clicked into place in Darby's brain so surely she could almost hear it. The answer was so simple; she couldn't believe she hadn't thought of it before.

She was a ghost from another time.

Strangely enough, the first thing this reminded Darby of was an old book on the Inuit she had found at the library. Inside the front page was a photograph. At the time, she'd figured the book publishers wanted to protect the picture, because they had inserted a really fine piece of paper over it. The librarian had called it onionskin. She felt like that onionskin. Thinner than paper, she fit between the centuries like she wasn't even there.

But of course she was there. And since she wasn't really ready to examine the whole onionskin/ghost thing too much, maybe it was time to quit thinking and start looking around. Why not? It's what Gabe had suggested, after all. The captain and his big goon hadn't seen her. She cast no shadow. That should mean she was free to roam around where she liked. Only one way to test out the theory, of course.

She decided to try it.

There wasn't a cloud in the sky, but when Darby stood on deck she could see where the surface of the water was all stirred up. To one side of the ship lay a dark line on the horizon. She wondered if it could be land.

But in order to find out which land in particular, she needed to do some investigating. Darby started by turning slowly in a circle, checking out everything within her range of vision. The ship was huge, with two big masts and square sails. There appeared to be some other small sail rigged to the front, though she couldn't see it clearly from where she stood. The deck was very broad, and there seemed to be at least two or three levels open to the air.

For a sunny day on such a big boat there was hardly anyone around. What she really needed was to find a quiet place to plant herself beside a group of chatty sailors. She snuck around to one side of the ship, but the only sailor she could see nearby was a man who was slowly climbing up the rigging near one of the big white sails, puffed full of wind and straining against the ropes holding it in place. Unlike Gabe, the sailor didn't seem to be talking to himself, and Darby wasn't about to risk her neck by climbing up there after him, anyway. She carried on with her careful tour.

Following a little further around one side of the deck, the wind dropped away, protected by the middle part of the ship. Darby almost tripped over a young couple, taking shelter in a corner between a pair of old barrels jammed up against the side rails. She pushed herself back against the wall, chiding herself for making such an unobservant ghost.

The couple had been hard to see because they had wrapped themselves in an old wool blanket, threadbare to the point of having huge holes all over it. The blanket was grey with grime and it looked like it might even be damp. Not the greatest protection from the elements.

When she crept up beside their little shelter, Darby could see they had the blanket rigged to stop the breeze from ruffling some paper the man was balancing on his knees. He held the paper with one hand, and the woman's head was pressed very close to his own as they sat on the deck. She had her hand on his arm.

"Pádraig, you know how important this is. It is too late for us now, but they must know the truth."

At the sound of her words, Darby knew at once why Gabe's voice had sounded so different. With everything else that was going on, she hadn't been able to pinpoint it, but it all came clear with the sound of this woman's voice. Gabe's accent had changed. All the French intonations were gone and now he sounded like this lady, and this man.

The man sighed and pulled a tiny black bottle out of his pocket. "I know you to be right, Alice-girl, but what will we say? Things are so bad at home in Sligo, to tell them all of how they are here will only take away the last shred of hope they may have."

She clenched his arm more tightly and Darby could see her pale face flush a little. "Mam's gone now, Pádraig, and if Da thinks that sending them away on the ships will mean a better life for the small ones, he will do what he can to get them aboard." She shook his arm a little. "They must not come, brother. Not until the transport is safer."

"I've heard tell the American ships are better," he said. He tried to say something else, but was overcome by a fit of coughing. A look of alarm crossed the woman's face and she helped him smother the coughs in the blanket.

Darby edged away a little. Could ghosts catch cold? She didn't want to learn the hard way.

By that time he had stopped coughing, but his eyes were streaming. Darby could see a little blood on the blanket where he had wiped his mouth. Just what kind of a cough was it, anyway?

"The American ships would not take us to Sligo," she said. "The price of the passage was far too dear and our landlord only had enough coin for our fares on the *Elizabeth*."

"Or so he claimed," said Pádraig, and his mouth twisted bitterly.

She picked up the small bottle from where he had dropped it, pulled the lid off and held it out to him. From an inside pocket he pulled out a slim wooden stick with a bit of a metal point stuck on one end and dipped it into the bottle.

"If they would not have us, they will not take the others. Now, say the words as you put them down, brother," the woman said urgently. "I want to be sure we make everything clear."

Things were starting to make sense for Darby, at last. Not a married couple, then, but a brother and sister, writing a letter home. And from their accents, home must be Ireland—or maybe Scotland. Darby had trouble telling the difference sometimes. She leaned in a bit closer to listen.

The woman closed her eyes. "You know, odd it may be, but I swear that as I think of home right now I can smell the apple trees in bloom." She opened her eyes and looked at her brother. "Do you think we'll ever see them, again, Pádraig? Or smell the scent of the laurel in the spring?"

"It feels to me that I'll never get the stink of this

ship out of my nose," he said bitterly. "I don't know what you are talking about, with all your nonsense about the scent of apples, Alice. Let's just get this letter written and be quit of it."

She dropped her head a little and nodded. "You are always so sensible, brother. I know in my heart we will never make the passage back to Ireland again, but perhaps there will be apples in the British colonies?"

Darby nodded to herself. Ireland, after all.

He smiled at her then, and squeezed her in a bit of a hug. "All right, Alice, I will pray there are apples, if only to still your talking of them for a while. Now, how shall we begin?"

He dipped his pen and wrote across the top of the page. Darby leaned forward and puzzled out the words upside down: *Aboard the* Elizabeth, *August 1847.*

He looked at Alice expectantly.

"*Dearest Da,*" Alice said immediately. "*Alice and myself are well and happy.*"

"You want to say we are happy? I don't feel very happy, Alice. I thought we were going to tell him the truth about the passage on this dreadful ship."

"We are, we are, but if he thinks *we* are safe, he will at least rest easy in his heart for us. Just write it down."

Pádraig obediently scratched a few words onto the page. "I do not even know if we can trust the captain to put this in with the post," he muttered, dipping his pen again.

"I will give it to that cabin boy. He will ensure it travels well to make it home to Da," Alice said.

Pádraig shook his head. "Do not put your hopes in the boy," he said softly. "I saw him sent below decks just after dawn this morning and have not seen him again since."

"Perhaps he has not sickened. It may be only the rough waves as we neared land that made him ill." Her voice was hopeful, but she stopped speaking when she looked into his face.

"Ay, durn't be a fool, Alice. His skin was dark. He has the black typhus just like the rest. He will be tossed overboard before two days have passed."

"But the *Elizabeth* will surely be in dock by then. The captain must value his crew, even if he treats his passengers so poorly. He will find a doctor to treat the boy when we are ashore."

The man lifted a hand to shade his eyes and looked out over the ocean. "I am not so sure we will reach land as soon as that. I believe there is a fair long sail up the St. Lawrence River before landing in Montreal."

Suddenly, a small child scampered along the deck, dragging a bit of broken wood as she ran. Alice leaned forward and called to her.

"Young Ellen—here! Come here, girlie."

The little girl changed direction and ran over, a grin splitting her face from ear to ear. She was missing at least four teeth and was wearing not much more than a bit of old sack. Still, she beamed happily at Alice and jumped onto her lap. Alice wrapped the corner of the blanket around the little girl.

"Hello, Mr. Pádraig," Ellen said shyly. Her lisp made it sound like "Mith-ter."

"Hello yourself, Miss Ellen," he said, smiling back at her.

Darby was smiling at her, too. She couldn't help it. The little girl was like a ray of sunshine. A dirty little ray, but all the same . . .

"What have ye been doing with yerself this morning, darlin' girl?" asked Alice.

"I've been staying out from under Mama's skirts," Ellen said as if she was reciting the words. "The new baby is all over spots, but Mama says I mustn't tell the crew." She looked thoughtful. "You won't tell the crew, will you, Miss Alice?"

Alice gave an alarmed glance at Pádraig. "What kind of spots, dear one?" she asked, her voice filled with worry.

But the little girl had caught sight of Pádraig's pen and ink. "Ohh—are you writing a letter? Mama says that in the colonies, when I am a big girl I will go to school and learn my letters."

"Yes, we are writing a letter home, but never mind about that now, Ellen. Tell me about the baby's spots. Is it a rash from his clout?"

Ellen shook her head. "No, no, no," she sang. "Not a rash on his bottie." She roared with laughter at the word.

Darby shook her head. This kid was as hard to

get information out of as Gabe. She watched as Alice took Ellen's dirty little face in her hands.

"Darling girl," she said. "Tell me about the baby's spots."

Ellen's eyes grew crafty. "Will you give me a sweetie if I do?" she asked Pádraig. "Mama says that the shops in Montreal are filled with sweeties."

"Yes, yes, I promise to give you a sweet in Montreal," said Pádraig. He was obviously less patient than Alice. "Just tell us about the damned spots."

Ellen smiled, her objective attained. "Did you see that man who got thrown in the ocean yesterday? Baby Sara has spots like those ones," she said in a matter-of-fact kind of way. "All bloody."

She jumped back to her feet and, still dragging her bit of wood, ran off again.

Pádraig folded his letter in two and slipped it into his pocket. "It's true, then," he said in a flat voice.

Alice struggled to her feet, and Darby slid down the wall a little to get out of her way. "It cannot be true," she cried. "The captain said it was contained. He said he kept that woman in strict quarantine. He locked her up, Pádraig. There is no way it could have gotten out." Her eyes filled with tears.

He shrugged. "And yet it has." He squinted his eyes, staring out at the strip of land coming ever nearer on the horizon. "Look how close we have come to our dream, Alice. Or perhaps it was only Da's dream—but he wanted it for us."

He stood up and put a hand on her arm. "There

will be no letter, unless it is a letter of goodbye, my dearest sister. We can keep our bodies washed with seawater and stay away from the holds where the lice that carry the typhus hide, but we cannot survive both typhus and the pox as well. From this day on, this ship carries none but the dead and those who wait to die."

He jammed his hands into the pockets of his threadbare trousers and left his sister leaning against the rail, weeping. Darby didn't know what to do. She trailed after Pádraig for a minute, but he turned and went down a set of rickety stairs. After what he had said about lice in the holds below, she didn't have any interest in following him.

The deck began to curve toward the front of the ship. As she walked around, Darby could see that the bow of the *Elizabeth* was open to the sky, and almost every plank of the deck was covered with passengers. People, mostly wearing clothing that made Gabe's rags look good, were sitting or lying around on the deck. Many were wrapped in threadbare blankets like Alice's. All around the edge of the open area were small ovens that had been built into the sides of the ship. Many of them had tiny fires going inside, which was pretty alarming when Darby thought about it, considering the boat was made of wood. What if a spark got out? The ovens themselves looked rickety, like someone had just hammered a few pieces of wood into place, slapped down some stones and called it a fireplace.

Behind Darby on the deck above, another group of crew members sat with their legs stretched straight out in front of them, working away on huge piles of sailcloth. They wore large thimbles strapped to their thumbs and sewed the cloth with some kind of strong thread. One crewman was standing off to the side with a coil of rope, carefully dipping the end into a bucket of some kind of thick, black goo.

She felt a breeze lift the back of her hair and turned to look out over the water. The sun was getting a bit lower on the horizon, and Darby realized that the afternoon had slipped away while she listened to Alice and her brother talk. The waves around the ship had little whitecaps on them and she had to grip the wooden handrail tightly to keep her balance. Some of the passengers were getting tossed around a bit, but no one showed any sign of wanting to put out the little fires. Darby could see jellyfish sailing along on top of the waves, looking like the caps of giant pink and purple mushrooms, floating on the sea.

She sidled up beside one small group, mostly because they were squabbling instead of just staring blankly at the sky like so many of the others.

"I'm hungry," wailed one of the children in the group. Darby was shocked to see a woman reach across the body of a sleeping man and slap the child hard in the face. "We're all hungry, Sammy," she snapped at him. "Now quiet down or ye'll wake himself, and you know what he'll do if ye snivel."

Darby shook her head in disbelief. This little trip was giving her a whole new appreciation of her own parents' disciplinary skills. She cast her eyes back to poor Sammy.

He had curled up in a ball, popped a thumb in his mouth and looked up at the sky. But his tears had an effect, after all. The mother, if she *was* Sammy's mother, dug her elbow into the ribs of the sleeping man. "Git yerself over, ya great lummox," she said. "The children are cryin' for their food. It's time for me to make the cakes."

The man snorted and rolled out of the way, only to go back to sleep in what looked like the most uncomfortable position possible, face down on the hard deck. He didn't even have a rag for a pillow. The woman got to her feet and marched over to some kind of hatch flipped open on the deck. She yelled something down the hatch, and presently a man came stumping up a nearby set of stairs with a wooden crate in his arms.

This created quite a stir on the deck as the passengers formed a quick, untidy line in front of the man. Most of the women in the line held out their skirts or their aprons and he scooped a quantity of some kind of dried flour right onto their clothes. A couple of the passengers held out small wooden bowls and got their servings in those. Darby waited to see what else they would be eating, but the man just walked away. That was dinner? A handful of dry flour?

Several quarrels began to break out around the deck, and Darby realized the passengers were fighting over their food. The so-called cakes that most of the families ate were nothing more than the flour mixed with a little water and baked on rusty iron pans. From her vantage point they looked pretty much like small pancakes, burnt on the outside and raw on the inside. No fruit or vegetables to be seen, or even milk. Maybe the cook handed those things out in the morning?

The main deck was now crammed full, more passengers having staggered up from their berths downstairs, so Darby scrambled over to the ladder leading to the deck above, where many of the sailors were watching the events down below. Some were even laughing, and she got the feeling that for some reason they didn't see the passengers as real people at all.

Gabe sat over to one side, well away from the other crewmen. The giant Alec was nowhere to be seen, and Gabe made a quick gesture to Darby. She ran around the edge of the deck, to keep as far as possible from the crew. It was windier up above, and from where Gabe sat, she couldn't hear the voices of any of the passengers or the crew at all.

"Put your knees up," Gabe hissed at her as she sat down beside him. She pulled the sailcloth over her knees, and hunched down underneath.

"If anyone sees me moving under this sheet, they really will think I'm a ghost," Darby whispered to him. He grinned and pulled the sailcloth right up over his head.

"It's meal time," he said in a low voice. "They'll all be busy for at least an hour—the passengers eating and fighting and the crew watching and laughing. We're as safe to talk here as anywhere."

"Where's the rest of the food?" Darby asked.

He shrugged. "That is all they have. The cook hands out half a pound of cornmeal for every adult, twice a day in the morning and evening. Sometimes he has bread, so they get that instead of the meal. There used to be a barrel of water with an iron cup they all shared, but since supplies have been running low, the cook doles that out, too."

"And they cook their food in those fireplaces?"

Gabe nodded. "Yes—they are stoves, really. Specially built for the passengers. The captain said that food was to be provided for crew only—passengers were to look after themselves. But so many boarded without any food at all, he's been forced to give out the cornmeal so they don't starve."

"I can't believe they don't starve, even with the cornmeal," Darby said. "No wonder everyone looks so weak and sleepy."

Gabe twitched the sailcloth aside, and she could see that the few remaining crew members were climbing down the ladder. "Some of the passengers boarded with small containers of herring, and one man even had a little bacon, but anything extra was gone within the first week. The rations are even less for the children, and I've seen mothers and fathers go hungry so that their children can at least have a bite of the burnt bits of cake they make in the ovens."

Darby wriggled around to make herself as comfortable as she could on the hard surface of the wooden deck. "This is just terrible," she said. "I've walked around a lot today and I've figured a bit of it out, but I still have a million questions."

"Why does that not surprise me?" he said, and his face crinkled a little. Darby could see that it hurt him to smile.

"I don't understand why you are going through this, Gabe," she said, pointing at the bruise on the side of his face. "That man really hurt you."

"Ah, but if it wouldn't make me red as a beet, I'd show you my ribs," he said jokingly. "They are all the colours of the rainbow after my taste of Alec's big boots."

"Quit joking around, you idiot," Darby said. "This seems like it could be dangerous to you—it *is* dangerous to you," she amended.

"We'll handle that sort of question later, thank you very much," he said, but at least his tone was more serious. "Now, why don't you tell me what you've learned on board today?"

So she did. Darby related the whole Pádraig and Alice tale, and all about Ellen and her baby sibling. He sat quiet, listening.

"I know this ship is sailing to Canada," Darby concluded. "But I don't know why. The people are from Ireland, that much I know. Pádraig said he was from Sligo."

"Some are from Sligo, which is a port town in Ireland, but most are farmers who worked on the land until it failed them," he said quietly. "Part of the problem was that the people of Ireland had a massive crop failure, and because they relied so much on that crop, there was a terrible famine."

The light from the setting sun shone red through the white sailcloth, and Gabe leaned over on one elbow.

"Was it potatoes?" Darby asked.

"Yes. Potatoes were a crop that grew very well in Irish soil—so well that many farmers grew nothing else. In the fall, the farmers began to dig up their crops. In some places, the blight didn't spread until the potatoes were all in the storage bins. It was a terrible disaster. One day they would have stored a full crop and the next day they would find their crop was nothing but black and rotting mush. In typical damp Irish conditions, one bad potato could infect a whole crop."

"Why didn't they just grow something else?"

"Things just didn't move that fast at the time. They had no ability to change crops quickly. Most of the farmers didn't even know about crop rotation to protect the soil. So they planted again, and prayed to God. When the second crop went bad, many people began to starve."

"But was there no other food in Ireland?"

Gabe looked at Darby steadily. "There was," he said quietly. "Barley, rye and even wheat. But many of the landlords of Ireland were Englishmen and they had the other crops earmarked for markets in Europe and at home in England. They would lose their profits if the food went to feed hungry people who could not pay."

"So it was cheaper to get rid of the problem people by sending them away?"

"Look around," he said. "What do you think?"

Darby peeked out from under the sailcloth, but all the crew members had gone somewhere else. To eat, maybe. The sky was a deep indigo blue—and the stars! She had no idea there were so many stars in the sky. She climbed out from under the cloth to stand against the railing and take a few deep breaths of the night air. With every second, the deep shades of blue drained out of the sky, leaving it black and star-filled. It was a wonder to see.

Most of the passengers had finished eating, and had curled up right on the deck to go to sleep. As the ship sailed on in the dark, the waves off to each side glowed a weird sparkling green against the black ocean. Darby felt Gabe come stand beside her.

"The radiance in the water is from the algae," he said in a low voice. "When they are disturbed by the passage of the ship, each tiny creature shines a light and together they make the ocean glow." He touched her arm and pointed her back to the spot under the sailcloth.

"We are better to stay under there," whispered Gabe. "Voices carry more in the night over water, and the captain has been setting a watch to make sure we don't get secretly boarded."

"Secretly boarded?" Darby pulled the cloth back over her head. It was no warmer underneath. She still couldn't get used to feeling so cold all the time. "Who is going to board a ship in the middle of the ocean?"

He shrugged. "I know it sounds unlikely, but the captain wants nothing to get in the way of completing his passage to Montreal. He pocketed the price for each passenger upon boarding, and he doesn't get extra for delivery. He wants to be quit of them and pick up whatever cargo awaits him there. And though you may not have seen any other ships today, there are many of them out there. Some are rife with diseases like smallpox and typhoid. If a ship's company runs out of food, who knows what they will try to do in desperation."

"Smallpox," Darby said slowly. "That must be what the baby has."

Gabe nodded. "Fifteen souls were lost mid-voyage before the crew of the *Elizabeth* managed to stem the outbreak. But perhaps one or two passengers concealed their symptoms, or perhaps the disease passed through clothes not burned when they should have been."

"They burn the clothes?"

Gabe sighed and sat up a bit. "The crew are deathly afraid of the pox. It is worse even than typhus. It can spread throughout a ship like wildfire, killing everyone aboard in a matter of a few days. So the captain has the crew throw anyone with symptoms of the disease over the side, some even before they have succumbed to the illness. Or, if he is feeling very generous, he will lock them in a room for the duration of the passage. Those who survive are released at the end of the journey. But usually none survive. The clothes of the dead are supposed to be tossed over the side or burned. But as you can see, these people are so poor, they sometimes hide the clothes and douse them in seawater hoping to kill the pox."

"Does that work?"

"No, of course not. And so the disease might stay dormant for a while before flaring up again. My guess is that is what has happened here."

Darby was quiet a moment. How many lives had been lost on this ship? And how many ships like this one had sailed away from Ireland?

Just as she opened her mouth to ask, Gabe disappeared. Or more accurately, a pile of sailcloth was unceremoniously dumped on her head and someone yanked Gabe out by the arm.

"'Ere's the little rat, then! It's yer turn on watch, bog boy. Mind you don't fall asleep on the job. Shirkers make good fish food."

Darby waited a moment or two before sliding out from under the cloth. In the moonlight, she could see Gabe climbing the rigging. He must have to do his watch in the crow's nest—the tiny platform at the top of one of the masts. It was so high, she lost sight of him when the dark seemed to swallow him halfway up the mast. Darby turned away and made a bed in the sailcloth, tucked tightly into one corner of the deck. Since there didn't appear to be any immediate chance to make her way home, she at least wanted to ensure no one would step on the *Elizabeth*'s newest resident ghost while she caught a few hours of sleep.

Chapter Ten

Darby awoke with the sun on her face and the strange feeling that she had forgotten to help Nan with something. *Am I late for dinner?* In this strange, timeless world it was hard to tell where she should be, or when she should be there. What about Gabe? How could the guy be in two places at once? And why was he the only person who could see her?

But since what she could do about this was exactly nothing, she decided to worry about it later. Suddenly she was not so sleepy anymore. The sun was shining and it was another beautiful day, but she was still cold. Sleeping under the sailcloth all night had done nothing to keep her warm, and the sun just wasn't doing its job now, either. She looked down at her fingers and noticed that the tips were stark, yellow-white.

Kinda like the fingers of a dead person.

Or a ghost.

She gave herself a little shake. Dark-side Darby thinking the worst again. She decided to go find Gabe.

She spotted him immediately after standing up. He was surrounded by passengers and other crewmen down on the main deck. It looked like there was a problem. Darby started down the ladder, but halted in her tracks as she took her first look at the ocean.

It seemed that overnight the *Elizabeth* had pulled further into an enormous river. She could see shoreline on both sides of the ship, but it was the front view that caught her eye. At least four ships lined up in the river, each anchored only a few hundred yards behind the one ahead. She scampered over to the rear part of the rail surrounding the upper deck. Sure enough, at least one ship was pulled in behind the *Elizabeth*, its deckhands scrambling to drop an anchor into the sea. There may have been more in the misty distance.

Darby decided the shoreline she could see on either side of the ship had to be Canada. Or whatever Canada was before it was a country. From the ship, the land looked like an endless, unbroken line of trees—dark and impenetrable. She thought of Mirkwood from *Lord of the Rings* and shivered a little. She couldn't see any sign of a city or even a docking place. This land looked nothing like the friendly place Darby called home. It looked dark and strange and dangerous.

She turned her gaze back to the ship, but there was no one to be seen on the open part of the main deck. This was odd because there seemed to be so many people on board; usually every open space was filled. Whatever was happening in front must be drawing a standing-room-only crowd.

With all the people missing, Darby watched as a rat made his leisurely way along the wooden handrail. He must have crawled out of one of the open hatches leading to the storage area under the ship. He was *not* a skinny rat. Darby guessed Gabe wasn't the only food thief on board.

Heading back to the foredeck, it took a minute or two to climb down the ladder. Darby had a little trouble getting around Alec's large feet without stepping on them. She managed to work her way up close to the front of the group. Gabe stood to one side of the captain, arms full of scraps of wood and brick. He raised his eyebrows in her direction.

The captain was in conversation with a man she didn't recognize. Of course, the *Elizabeth* was filled with men Darby didn't recognize, but this man was different. For one thing, he was clean. He wore grey pants that had sharp creases down the front and a matching vest and coat. Even the cloth tied around his neck looked like it had been freshly ironed.

She couldn't really see his face, as he was wearing thin, grey gloves and holding an enormous handkerchief over his nose and mouth. This also made it quite difficult to understand what he was saying. The captain's face was bright red from bellowing at the man. From the part of his face Darby could see, the man looked pretty exasperated as well.

Finally he stepped away from the captain, so that he was practically leaning backwards over the rail, and pulled the cloth from his face.

"My good man," he said in a voice that carried far more clearly, "there is simply no reason to shout at me. I am merely delivering the news as it was relayed to me by the doctor at the quarantine station on Grosse-Île. If you trouble yourself to gaze both fore and aft, you will see that yours is not an isolated problem. Two days ago I marked the number of ships awaiting inspection at more than forty. Today there are probably three times that number."

The captain stepped forward and brandished something in the man's face. It looked like some kind of spyglass. "Now you need to listen to me, Mr. Driscoll, or whatever it is that you call y'self. What *you* don't understand, sir, is that I 'ave a full complement of raw lumber awaiting me in Quebec City. Every day that I am late to pick up that shipment, I pay a penalty to me agent in Liverpool."

He gestured around at the silent group of people listening to the exchange. "These passengers are just cargo I took on so as not to travel across the Atlantic with an empty 'old. They is not me principle occupation, nor me concern once we make land."

Oh, nice, thought Darby. The passengers were less valuable than a bunch of wood? The captain's reputation wasn't going up in her opinion.

One of the women stepped forward and plucked at Driscoll's sleeve.

"If there is illness on board, sir, will it slow our passage into the colonies?"

Driscoll stepped hastily away from the woman, almost tripping himself in his hurry. He put the handkerchief back up over his mouth, and his voice muffled again. "Indeed, madam. There is a quarantine of a minimum of fifteen days if the doctor confirms illness is present."

He removed the cloth from his mouth for a moment and looked sharply at the captain. "Surely your complement of passengers includes more than just Irish?"

The captain shook his head. "Not that it is any concern of yours, but I took this whole load on in Sligo. Passage west fully paid. What 'appens to them in the colonies is nobody's business but their own."

Driscoll looked across the group of silent faces and then back at the captain. "I hope you will convey to these poor souls that unless they have a trained skill, the Irish are as welcome in the colonies as stray dogs." He sniffed a little. "Have you any evidence of typhus or the pox aboard, sir?"

The captain shook his head firmly. "None, sir. Ye can be sure of that." His eyes took on a crafty look that reminded Darby of little Ellen. "P'raps it is simply a matter of a financial incentive to speed our progress past the quarantine regulations? If ye would just accompany me down to my cabin, I'm sure we can come to an agreeable arrangement."

Driscoll swung one leg over the handrail and

perched precariously on the side of the ship. For the first time, Darby noticed a smaller craft—not much bigger than a large rowboat—was tied up, bobbing in the waves alongside the *Elizabeth*. He tucked his handkerchief into his pocket.

"Captain Cameron," he said severely, "I will do you the honour of not reporting your words. In these terrible days, bribery is a treasonous offence. And I most certainly will not descend to your reeking cabin, but will immediately take my leave. I have several more ships to board this day, and as I have no further business here, I bid you adieu."

With those words, he swung his other leg over the side and half-slid down a rough rope ladder that the men in his boat below must have rigged up earlier. The passengers and crew watched in silence as six men on the small craft took up oars and began paddling for all they were worth in the choppy ocean. It looked like they were aiming for the ship that was anchored behind the *Elizabeth*.

The woman who had stepped forward before turned to the captain. "What are your plans now, Cameron? Ye may be more than a few days late to pick up yer precious cargo."

Other voices began to call out, including shouts of "Give us food!" and "Tell those below that no sickness is aboard!" The passengers began to push each other in an effort to get close enough to the captain so he would hear their complaints.

Gabe caught Darby's eye and gestured toward a

nearby doorway, so she shoved through the jostling crowd and followed him in the door.

The area was little more than a storage closet and, crammed full of assorted bits of sail and rope, it felt about as roomy as the inside of Darby's locker at school. Gabe managed to cram the door shut against the crowd outside, and they faced each other practically nose to nose with some kind of a rusty block-and-tackle arrangement jammed between them.

"Okay, look," Darby said as soon as he got the door closed. "Just exactly what did you mean when you said this place isn't safe? You've been punched out at least once since I've been here. And the last thing I want to do is arrive back in your garden carrying some kind of horrible disease that no one has ever heard of. I mean, what the heck is typhus? And how about smallpox—is it just a smaller version of chicken pox?"

Gabe shook his head. "I'm afraid not," he said, almost yelling over what sounded like some kind of a riot going on outside the door.

"Well, I'm worried," Darby yelled back. "I want to find out what happened to these people—to Alice and Pádraig and little Ellen. But I also don't want to make my grandparents sick, and I don't particularly like the sound of any of these conditions for myself, either."

"You needn't worry about the illness," he said. "Being a traveller such as yourself means that you *are* at risk, no doubt. While your presence has very little impact on the solid objects of this era, you can still be hurt. If an iron bar came crashing down on your head or you if fell into a pit of tigers, you would have trouble on your hands, make no mistake. Animals are a particular risk; they don't rely on vision as much as people do, and your presence is more evident to them. This is why I stay with you, to keep you safe from iron bars and tiger pits and to make sure you get back home in one piece. No one knows you are here. You are as much a part of the room as the furniture—no more."

Darby's exasperation rose up. "So, I should think of myself as a couch or maybe a toilet?" she snapped.

"A toilet?" he said.

She stared at him a minute and then they both laughed.

"It's just so hard to know what to do when you won't give me all the information," she said.

He shrugged. "I don't have time for a long explanation here. Just know that disease and such is no danger to you, for while you are *in* this time, you are not *of* it."

Great. Like that made a lot of sense. But compared to the fact that this ghost-from-another-time affliction wouldn't have protected her from that polar bear, it was at least on the good news side of the spectrum.

Suddenly, there was a tremendous explosion right outside the door. Darby grabbed Gabe's arm in terror. "What was that?"

"I believe it was a gunshot," he said calmly.

"A gunshot? It sounded more like a cannon going off to me," she said. As soon as her ears stopped ringing, she pushed past Gabe and tried to peek outside through a crack in the door. She could feel him craning over her shoulder to look.

"You smell like apples," he whispered.

"It's my shampoo," she hissed back, thinking of Alice. "Do you think they can . . . ?"

But the captain started to shout and his voice drowned her out.

As they peeked through, they could see Captain Cameron stood with his back to the door and beside him was one of his crewmen. Gabe had been right—he held some kind of a shotgun. A little smoke was still coming out of the gun, both the barrel and the back near where he must have lit a fuse or something.

"This section of the afterdeck be for the crew ONLY," he roared. "The penalty for crossing the line I have drawn will be the loss of a day's ration of water. A full inspection of all the passengers will commence immediately. Mr. Damian, if you please."

Gabe's tormentor, Alec, stepped forward. "*He's* Mr. Damian?" Darby whispered.

Gabe nodded. "Believe it or not, he's the ship's dentist. I think he got the job because he was the strongest man on board for pulling out bad teeth."

"Either that or he enjoyed it the most," she muttered. "That was one big shotgun."

Gabe slid the door shut again as the passengers began to disperse. "It is a musket, actually. A flintlock musket."

Darby knew that. She remembered seeing one in a movie her social studies teacher had shown on the Civil War.

"What do you think they are going to do now?"

Gabe actually looked a little worried. "This is a tenuous time," he said in a low voice. "I think perhaps you have seen enough."

"What does that mean?" Darby asked, feeling her exasperation rise again. She had hardly seen anything, and her questions outnumbered any answers by at least ten to one.

"It means I need to show you the way home," he said firmly. He took Darby's shoulders and pushed her out through the door. Most of the people were gone from this part of the deck, and she could see the line the captain had drawn on the dirty surface of the boards with a piece of chalk.

Gabe hauled her around to the foredeck. There were a few passengers scattered about, but most had disappeared. "Where is everybody?" she hissed.

They stopped in front of the first fireplace. It was full of cinders and burnt wood, but was not in use. Gabe leaned against the wooden frame that supported the rickety oven.

"Everyone has gone below. We must move quickly before they return. This stone hearth is your portal. Just crawl . . ."

But before he was able to finish, there was a desperate scream from the stairwell beside them.

Gabe took a step toward the stairwell and tripped

a little as the stone from the hearth shifted and caught the toe of his boot. "Wait here," he whispered, and ran for the top of the stairs. Darby tried to shove the rock back into place, but it broke and a piece came off in her hand. She stuffed it into her pocket, making a mental note to replace it as soon as she had a chance.

A moment later, Gabe was backing away from the stairs, his arms raised high over his head. Out of the stairwell emerged the scary end of the musket, and it was pointing straight at Gabe. Soon enough, the other end of the musket showed up, clutched in the hands of Gabe's buddy, Mr. Damian. Behind him, a crew member was struggling up the stairs with a bundle in his arms. The reason he was struggling was that he also had a woman clawing at him—his arms, his clothes, whatever she could reach. She clearly was trying to get her property back.

As the group of them tumbled onto the deck, Darby could see the woman had a little girl running behind her. The woman continued to scream and the little girl was crying and trying to cling to her mother's skirt.

It was Ellen.

Alec Damian pointed the musket at various people in the crowd that was starting to gather. No one seemed anxious to see him use it. The captain emerged from below, and neatly plucked the bundle from the hands of the crew member. A look of disgust on his face, he turned and shook the thing at the woman.

"This is AGAINST the rules," he roared, his face purple with rage. The bundle was wrapped with some grimy lace that perhaps once had been white but was now a grey and matted mess. The captain shook the bundle so hard the lace came free, and to Darby's horror, she saw a tuft of reddish-blond hair.

It couldn't be.

It was.

A baby—tinier than Darby had ever seen.

Ellen's mother screamed again. She seemed to be beyond words. Ellen clung to her leg, crying uncontrollably.

"Damian. Get me a bit o' that cloth," the captain snarled. The large man grasped a section of sail from the pile about to be mended and, with a mighty flex of his arms, ripped a piece of the fabric away.

Cameron laid the small bundle on the piece of cloth, and the thin wrappings around it fell away. The air was suddenly completely still. The captain turned slowly toward the crowd of passengers and his face changed, somehow.

"I am not a monster," he said, his voice shaking with emotion. "This will be done as best we are able. But Missus Donnelly, ye have ta know that keeping this bairn on board will mean nothing but death for the rest of us. The child is long dead, woman."

Darby could not tear her eyes off the baby. Every square inch of the tiny body was covered in blisters. Between the fingers and toes, all through the hair—it was the worst thing she had ever seen in her life. On the torso, most of the blisters were flattened, but she could see where many of them had filled with blood. The face had no features at all. It just looked like a solid black mask. The baby's eyes were open and what should have been the whites of the eyes were also filled with blood. There were even blisters on the tongue, which was swollen right out of the mouth.

The captain pulled the cloth across the little body and the baby's mother stood up. She was still held tightly in the grip of the crew member, but she had somehow found her voice.

"'Tis only that I wanted her buried on consecrated ground, Captain," she said, and Darby could see what the words were costing her. Sweat stood out across her forehead, and her face was ashen grey. Darby could also see a rash of red blisters on the inside of her forearms. "I didn't want my Sara cast over the side like the others, without the words of a priest to see her wee soul to heaven. Please," her voice faltered, "please. I will keep her safe, away from the rest of the passengers. You have my word. You may lock me up as you did the others. Just let my baby be sent on her journey by a priest, Captain."

Darby felt a wave of weakness wash over her at the sight of the tiny body, and had to lean against the wall so she didn't fall down. The hundreds of passengers continued to watch in utter silence, and even Ellen stopped wailing.

Cameron jerked his head at another of his crewmen, who dragged a plank of wood across the deck.

The captain, far more gently now, lay the tiny limp bundle on the plank and quickly swaddled it in the rough sailcloth. Darby could see his hands tremble as he covered the dead child's face.

"I'm afraid I cannot agree to your request, Missus Donnelly," he said. "The risk is too great."

The baby's mother collapsed completely, weeping, at the captain's feet.

Suddenly the captain turned to Pádraig. "You," he said roughly. "Yer a teacher, are you not? You must 'ave some Latin. Give us a few words to speed this wee babe on its journey."

Alice was clutching her brother tightly by the hand, but she let go and he stepped toward the captain. Darby heard him start to say what sounded like the words of a prayer, and as he did, the captain tied the sailcloth tightly in place around the bundle with a length of leather lacing. Alice reached over and put an arm around Ellen, who was still crying softly at her mother's side.

Darby had been leaning back against the wooden door of the storage closet, and she was aware of Gabe, still beside her. "This way," he breathed in her ear, and as the captain picked up the bundle, they slipped around the edge of the foredeck.

"Wait," Darby whispered, as he propelled her along. "I just need to know they will be all right."

He stopped and looked her in the face. "A few will be," he said in a low voice. "But your time here is done."

Over his shoulder she could see the captain move to the rail with the bundle in his arms. He turned to the baby's mother, and Darby was surprised to see tears rolling down his face. "I know what's in your 'eart," he said to Mrs. Donnelly. "One of me own 'as made this journey, you may remember."

Darby looked at Gabe. "His wife was one of the first stricken," he whispered. "She died little more than a week into the sailing." He put his hand on her head to protect her from bumping it on the stone fireplace.

As she knelt down, Darby watched the captain nod at his crewman, who lifted the plank of wood and tipped the tiny body over the side of the ship.

She didn't hear a splash.

But as the strange fog curled out of the stone hearth to take her, she watched the white and grey–clad form of Sara's mother break free of the crewman's arms and throw herself, like a swooping gull, over the side of the ship to join her baby. And the last sounds Darby heard were Ellen's screams.

Chapter Eleven

Darby lay on the grass and stared up at the sky, her face covered in tears and her head pounding like the percussion section of the school orchestra.

When Gabe had sweet-talked her onto the window ledge, she'd forgotten about the headache. But it hadn't forgotten her, and it was back, in all its pain-wracked, Technicolor glory.

She tried to think about something else to push the pain away. The problem was she didn't want to think about where she had just been or what she had just witnessed. The tiny baby's blackened face was the worst thing Darby had ever seen in her life. But at least the baby's pain was over. The pain in her mother's face and in her sister's screams . . . Darby knew they would live on in her memory forever.

She couldn't help it—she just lay there and cried. For Ellen, who, if she even survived the journey, would be an orphan in a strange land. For Pádraig and Alice, who had pinned all their hopes on moving to a place that, if

Driscoll was right, valued them less than stray dogs. And, if forced to admit it, she cried a bit for herself, too. She didn't want to have seen what those people went through. She didn't want to know.

Too late. The damage was done, as her mother would say. Dark-side Darby seeing the worst, as usual. But what else was there to see?

This made her sit up. In spite of the headache, one thing was perfectly clear. This wasn't just Darby looking at the dark side. These things had really happened. Alice and Pádraig and Ellen's mother had lives so awful, they had risked everything to come to Canada.

Strangely enough, as she wiped her tears away, she found the headache easing a little. She could still feel where the axe had been planted behind her right eye, but it was like somebody had pulled it out, and was maybe just taking a breather before swinging it into her brain again. She curled back over on her side and breathed in the scent of the fragrant grass of Gabriel's garden. The pain might be easing, but the awful pictures were still there. Starving, ragged people, risking their lives and everything they had to come to a land that didn't want them. How would she ever forget the loss and pain in Ellen's voice?

Suddenly another voice was in her head. "Big Irish family," Fiona had said. "I can't keep them all straight."

Could Fiona's family have arrived in Canada on a ship like the *Elizabeth*? She had said her family was Irish. And if *her* family was Irish . . .

Darby rolled over onto her knees and carefully tried to stand up. The pain hovered behind her eyes and rattled around the inside of her skull a little, but it was so much easier than before, she wanted to cry with relief.

No more crying. There were questions to answer.

—⁓—

Darby walked in the front door to find Nan on the telephone. She still couldn't move her head very fast, but the worst of the headache was definitely gone. The whole way home she'd been going over cover stories to explain where she'd been, but . . .

"That's wonderful news, Allan. Do you want to want to speak with Darby? She's just walked in the door."

Nothing. Not even a "Where have you *been,* young lady?" Darby looked at her watch.

"Oh, Allan, I didn't know it was a secret. Of course I won't tell. That's for you and Sandra to decide."

4:00 p.m. Darby pushed the button to check the date.

"Lovely to talk with you, dear. Here's Darby!" She held out the phone.

July twenty-first.

She'd been gone for just a little more than an hour.

"Darby, dear—did you hear me? Your father is on the phone. He wants to say hello. Here you go, dear."

Nan passed the phone to Darby and she had a conversation with her dad of which, even seconds after she hung up, she could not remember a single word. She thought maybe he said the reno was going well. She thought he also may have said they had a surprise for her. She *knew* he told her when they were planning to arrive for a short visit before taking her home.

She just couldn't remember any of it.

Every fibre of Darby's being told her she had been away for two days on a ship in the Atlantic Ocean. With the minor added detail of the whole event happening in another century. But her watch and her grandmother's reaction indicated something completely different. So she did the only sensible thing possible under the circumstances.

Darby peeled potatoes.

After her dad said goodbye, Nan handed over the potato peeler and a bucket of spuds. One thing Darby had already learned—nothing is better for thinking than having to peel a big red wash bucket full of potatoes.

"Just a moment, young lady," Nan said sternly. "What is that you have jammed in your pocket?"

Darby looked down. Sure enough, the pocket of her cutoffs was sticking out like there was a potato in it. She reached inside.

"Uh—it's just a rock, Nan," Darby said, and pulled it out.

Not just any rock, though. It was the piece of hearthstone from the *Elizabeth* that Gabe had tripped over.

"Well, please don't carry big rocks around in your pocket like that. You might have ripped your shorts."

Darby carefully set the rock on the back stairs where she would remember to take it up to her room. Then she grabbed the bucket, the peeler and a sheet of *The Guardian* and took them out to the back porch. She wanted to let her hands do the work while her brain tried to sort out what had happened. She thought about the first trip to the frozen North. She thought about the second trip on the Atlantic Ocean.

And then she thought about something entirely different. Darby was a sceptic by nature. She clearly remembered the moment she figured out that bunnies were not biologically capable of laying chocolate eggs, and shortly after that, the moment she decided the hand replacing the tooth under her pillow with a toonie might not be coated in fairy dust. But this was not like those moments. In fact, this was the *opposite* of those moments. Instead of seeing life in the harsh light of reality, she had to talk herself into believing in magic.

Darby found herself in the very odd position, while peeling potatoes on her grandparents' back porch, of beginning to doubt her own doubts.

The cure for all of this could only be a few good, solid facts. And there was one place Darby had come to rely on when she needed information. Her plan for tomorrow was set. She needed to hit the library.

When Darby walked back into the kitchen with her big bowl of freshly peeled potatoes, Nan looked at her critically. "You *are* wearing that helmet when you ride your skateboard, aren't you?"

"Yes, Nan."

"Hm. I guess it can't do much to protect those shins of yours. You look like you've been crawling through broken glass," she said, gesturing at the scrapes on Darby's legs.

Darby had to admit they did look pretty bad.

"It worries me more that your eyes are still so red," Nan said. "Is your head aching again?"

"It was a bit sore today, but it's a lot better now," Darby said carefully. She didn't want to lie to Nan, but there was no way she wanted to share any wacko theories at this point—or admit she'd been crying.

"I think you need a little more rest," Nan said firmly.

"Well, I'm only planning to go to the library tomorrow. Nothing strenuous," Darby said.

"All right," Nan agreed reluctantly. "But only if you walk over. I want you to take a day away from riding that skateboard."

A one-day ban? No problem. Darby could live with that.

"Okay," she agreed, and went over to the sink to wash her hands.

The telephone rang again. Nan laughed. "My goodness. I hardly hear this thing all year, but now that you are here it seems to ring all the time."

She picked up the phone with a jolly "Hello!" but her face fell almost immediately. "Thank you, Ernie," she said quietly. "I'll get my bag and meet you right out front."

She hung up the telephone and Darby could see her trying to put on a cheerful face.

"What is it, Nan?"

"Oh, it's just your grandfather, up to his tricks again. I thought he was having a nap upstairs, but it turns out he was taking a little trip down to Province House."

She picked up her purse and headed for the front door.

"I'll come too," Darby said, and flipped off the switch on the stove burner under the potatoes.

"Thank you, dear," Nan said. "Between the three of us, I know we'll be able to persuade him to come home."

It was really only a couple of blocks to get to the big government building, so Ernie had them there in a flash. "I was just circling, looking to pick up a fare," he said to Nan, "when I saw him sitting by the cenotaph. I—I just thought it might be better if you came to get him."

Darby hopped out of the cab with Nan as soon as Ernie pulled over at a taxi stand, and she spotted Gramps right away. He was the only person standing beside the cenotaph in boxer shorts and undershirt.

"Oh, dear," she heard Nan say, under her breath. Darby knew this would be horrifyingly embarrassing for Nan, so she decided to put a different spin on it.

"We have pyjama day at school all the time and all the kids wear boxers," she said to her worried grandmother. "The more colourful, the better. Besides, half the guys wear their pants so low, their boxers are hanging out anyway." *It could have been a lot worse,* Darby thought. *Lucky he didn't sleep naked.*

"Hi Gramps," she said cheerfully, as she walked up to him. "Did you know that Nan's making garlic mashed potatoes for supper?"

Nan shot Darby a grateful look and they both reached over to take one of his hands. He had been staring at the names listed under the Korean Conflict, reaching up and running his fingers over them as he read them under his breath. When Darby spoke, his eyes were cloudy and distant, and he looked like he didn't have a clue who she was.

But at the sight of Nan, his eyes cleared. "Just thought I'd nip down to have a peek at the boys," he said gruffly and then caught sight of the cab. "What are you doing here, Ernie?"

Ernie slapped Gramps on the back. "Just cruising around, Vern. It's a slow day today. How's about you let me give you a lift home?"

"No need for that, Ernie. It's just a block or two if we cut through the lane."

"Darby is not feeling well," blurted Nan, suddenly. "I think it's better to accept Ernie's kind offer and get her home quickly."

Gramps bobbed his head immediately. "These young ones," he said to Ernie as he hopped in the front seat beside him. "No stamina. Let's get the kid home, Ern."

He leaned over the backseat to look at them. "I hear ye've got garlic mash on the menu, Etta. That so?"

Nan nodded at Gramps, then turned to smile at Darby. The drive home took all of two minutes, and Nan insisted that Ernie come in and enjoy roast chicken and mashed potatoes with the family.

Crisis averted. Gramps even appeared at the dinner table with his trousers on.

"It's lucky it's summer," Darby said, staring up at the indigo sky. She'd last seen a sky that colour when sailing

on a ship in a different century. The very thought made
her shiver a little.

Nan and Darby were sitting on the porch after dinner.
They had just waved goodbye to Ernie. Gramps was in
watching the news and guarding his remote from
teenage-girl invasion.

"I'm sure anyone who saw him thought he was just out
walking, wearing his shorts."

Nan arched an eyebrow at Darby. "Oh, yes. He com-
monly goes out in his blue-striped shorts with horses on
them."

Darby laughed a little. "Nan, you have got to get
Gramps up to speed with today's fashion. Blue stripes are
so last year. This year everyone will only be seen in green
stripes with horses."

Nan laughed a little, too, which made Darby happy.
She was more concerned about Nan at the moment
than she was about Gramps. He'd be okay. For a while,
anyway.

Nan sat beside Darby with her medicine-in-a-sherry-
glass. She'd even broken down and let her granddaughter
have a Coke.

"But the caffeine is so bad for you, dear," she'd wailed.
Darby grinned. Half the kids in her class would've been
sneaking the sherry, for Pete's sake.

But Nan had caved and the two of them were sitting
in the screened porch so they could enjoy the night air
without being eaten alive. Darby had been given official
flyswatter duty, but so far they'd managed to keep them all
outside the screens.

"You're not up playing your new video game," said Nan, sipping her sherry.

"You said I can't drink Coke in my room," Darby reminded her.

Nan grinned an evil little smile. "We old grannies have ways of keeping our granddaughters nearby," she said.

Darby laughed. "I was just kidding, anyway. It was really nice of Fiona to give me that stuff. My wrists are still a little sore from playing with it so much the other day."

She spotted a fly that had made it in past the screen and introduced it to eternity with the swatter.

"That Fiona is a lovely girl," said Nan when Darby sat down. "I'd almost forgotten about the connection between our families."

"Yeah, it's kind of cool having a sort-of cousin I didn't even know about."

"When family names change it makes it hard to keep track." Nan suddenly looked at her granddaughter sharply. "You do know my maiden name, don't you dear?"

Talk about putting a person on the spot. Darby thought fast.

"Um—is it Urquhart?" she said, flailing wildly.

Nan laughed. "Nice guess, but that's your grandfather's family, dear. No—it's Darby."

Her granddaughter looked at her blankly. "Darby? Your name was Etta Darby?"

"It still is," she said. "Or rather, it is Etta Darby Christopher. I am the youngest of three girls, my dear, and by the time I was born, they couldn't be bothered to think up a middle name for me. So when I married, I kept my maiden name as my middle name. And when you were born, I think your mother liked the sound of it, and here you are."

"Wow," Darby said, and she meant it. "I'm kinda mad my mom and dad didn't tell me this before. I mean, it's so cool we share a name."

"It's Irish," said Nan, draining her glass. "My family, and Fiona's, of course, came to Canada after the great famine. My great-grandmother arrived on a coffin ship. Her name was Alice."

Darby knocked her Coke bottle over. "Alice? You're kidding me—her name was really Alice?"

"Let me just get a cloth for that, dear," Nan said. "I think I may have a refill, anyway." She opened the door and turned back absently. "You know, I've always loved the name Alice."

Darby's head practically exploded right on the spot. Could it be the same Alice? It was a common name. Every neuron in her brain began leaping fast and fierce, but before she could say a word, she noticed Nan's eyes had filled with tears.

"I'm sorry, Nan. It's only a couple of drops," Darby said, wiping up any evidence with the paper napkin Nan had handed her with the drink.

"Oh, it's not the spill, dear. Accidents happen in the best of regulated families." She smiled a little. "I was just remembering Alice."

As more evidence of how stunned Darby was feeling, she asked: "Did she die?"

Nan laughed a little at that brilliant remark. "Well, yes, she did die eventually, but not until she was an old lady. She was the only one in her family to survive the crossing from Ireland. I believe her brother made it over as well, but he died of tuberculosis shortly after they arrived. No, Alice lived a long life. She eventually married into another Irish family that was already living here on the Island. There were many Irish immigrants who came to Canada long before the great famine, but her story is as far back as I know within my own family heritage."

"Maybe I can find some records at the library tomorrow," Darby said quickly. "It would probably help if you could remember the name of the ship Alice came on . . ."

"I always loved the name Alice," Nan said wistfully. "I once—"

"Etta!" Gramps was bellowing from the living room. "Etta, the goddamned battery has fallen out of this remote and rolled under the chesterfield."

Nan slipped inside the house without another word.

A billion questions and not an answer to be had. It was as bad as talking with Gabe.

Darby slipped out the screen door, careful not to let a single member of the insect world get past her, and walked through the moon shadow cast by the oak tree in front of the house. The stars were a little less bright tonight than last, probably because a beautiful fingernail moon had risen. It hung like a white hammock in the sky, almost cradling the tiny gleam of Venus to one side.

Could it be the same moon that had shone down on Alice and Pádraig on their coffin ship? Darby hoped the kind librarian would help her find out.

Chapter Twelve

Darby soon discovered that searching for information about a time in the past is a whole lot easier when there is a written record. Over the next few days she realized that she had the opposite problem from her hunt for clues into the lives of the people of the North. When she looked up the Irish Potato Famine in the computer catalogue at the library, hundreds of entries came up. There was *way* too much information. How would she ever find out what happened to Alice and Pádraig and the rest of the passengers on the *Elizabeth?*

She spent a whole day looking at pictures of the coffin ships, including drawings and sketches of how cramped the quarters were below decks. People were crammed in like sardines. Darby remembered the awful smell that wafted up out of the stairwells and hatch covers. Every time she thought of little Ellen sleeping down there with her mother and the dead baby, her stomach clenched into a knot.

Reading the text that accompanied the pictures, Darby discovered that some people lived through smallpox because they had once been exposed to something called cowpox. In fact, it was through this connection that doctors finally figured out how to come up with a vaccine. Darby sat back in her seat with a sigh. So maybe Ellen had a chance of survival, after all.

She also learned that she was not the only one interested in looking at this information. The librarian, whose name tag said "Alfie," called them genealogists and pointed out hundreds of web sites on the computer that helped people trace their heritage.

Darby thought she had hit the jackpot when she found a web site listing ships that travelled out of Ireland during and after the famine, but after checking and rechecking the list, she still couldn't find the *Elizabeth* named anywhere.

"That doesn't mean it doesn't exist," said Alfie when Darby asked her. "The reason life aboard those ships was so terrible was that most of them weren't meant to carry people in the first place. They were supposed to carry cargo like coal or other minerals, and they just crammed the people on board to make extra money."

That had Captain Cameron written all over it. Darby remembered what he said about picking up lumber in Quebec. But it meant she might never find out about the people on the ship. Maybe she needed to buttonhole Nan for more details.

Darby signed out a few books for extra reading and hurried home. Since she was banned from the skateboard, she practised her balance by carrying the books on her head. She managed to make it almost all the way up the front steps with a big fat book (boringly entitled *Ireland in the Nineteenth Century*) on her head when Nan dashed past. She had something khaki-coloured in her hands, and it was smoking. Darby followed her into the kitchen to find her dousing Gramps's old military uniform in the sink.

"He got lost in a television program on Scotland," she said harriedly, "and he forgot he was in the middle of ironing his uniform."

Her hair was sticking up and she looked exasperated. "This is why I do the ironing around here, and don't you forget it!"

"Okay, Nan."

Since Darby hadn't ever ironed anything in her life, she figured that agreeing was a pretty safe bet. She also decided it might be a good time to make herself scarce, so she grabbed one of the coffin ship books and Nan's knobbly sweater to sit on, and headed out to the porch.

Several hours later, Darby was deep in the middle of copying out a passenger manifest from her book when Nan called from the kitchen.

"I sent Gramps out into the garden an hour ago for a handful of the last raspberries, and he hasn't come back in."

Visions of the cenotaph danced in Darby's head. "Do you think he's taken off, Nan?"

"No, dear, I know he's back there. I've been making pastry and I can see the gate from here, but I just hope he hasn't dozed off in the sun." She rolled her eyes. "You know how Gramps is about something like sunscreen. Stubborn doesn't begin to describe it."

"Okay, I'll go have a look."

Darby took the two glasses of lemonade that Nan pushed into her hands and elbowed her way out the screen door.

She paused on the step to take in the warmth of the day. It was strange—after the journey on the *Elizabeth,* the headache had been so much milder than the first time, but the cold wouldn't leave her, even with Nan's sweater. After staggering home from Gabe's back garden, it had taken at least half an hour under the shower to get warm. Unfortunately, this meant she used up all the hot water and Gramps had to yell for a while, just to get it out of his system. He seemed fine by breakfast the next day, though. Darby figured he'd forgotten all about it by then. Who said Alzheimer's didn't have its advantages?

Looking around the garden, at first glance Darby reckoned Nan must have blinked. There was no sign of Gramps anywhere in the backyard. Both of the big Adirondack chairs were empty and he wasn't in the garden, either. She was just going back in to report to Nan when something caught her eye near the raspberry bushes. It looked like a shoe.

Sure enough, when she peeked into the spot Gramps had shown her a few weeks earlier, there he was. Most of the berries were gone—either picked or dried up—so the area underneath formed a little hollow that couldn't really be seen from the house.

It was dim and leafy and cool under there, so Darby set down the glasses and crawled in herself.

"Hi, Gramps. Feel like a lemonade?"

"Sure thing, kiddo. Bring it on in."

"Uh—are you sure, Gramps? Wouldn't you rather drink it in your chair?"

"No, sir. It's like an oven out there, and if I sit in the sun, Etta will be after me to rub some of that stinking lotion on. Just bring it in here."

Darby crawled back out of the bushes and gave Nan a thumbs-up sign through the kitchen window, even though she felt a little anxious. She was not so worried about bringing him the drink, but she'd noticed he had two of his old scrapbooks with him and she didn't want to ever live through a repeat of the big argument.

She took a deep breath to steel herself before grabbing the glasses and a cork mat that had been sitting on the little table outside. Bending low, Darby passed them all through to Gramps in his raspberry cave.

When she crawled back inside, she saw that Gramps had managed to find the trunk of a tree to lean on. He looked pretty comfortable, but it was weird to see him there. Sort of like some wrinkled-up little boy, hiding in his fort.

Darby picked up her lemonade and prepared to knock it back in one gulp. Gramps had a faraway look in his eyes that she didn't like at all.

"Have ye ever found yourself in a situation you don't understand, kiddo? Where ye feel like a fish out of water?"

Darby darted a look at her grandfather, but his face was serene. She couldn't think of a better way to describe her summer than those very words. She took a sip of lemonade instead of a gulp, and sat back a little.

"You know," he said, "I was only twenty when I first saw combat, and I felt like a goddamned beached fish the whole time I was there."

The strange thing was, when Gramps described his experiences going to war, he sounded almost as freaked out as Darby had been over the past few weeks. She adjusted her position so as not to get poked in the side by a raspberry root and listened to him talk.

Darby didn't know Gramps had been a pilot. He told her about seeing all the soldiers coming back after the Second World War when he was a kid, and how it made him think guys in uniform were the bravest men on the planet.

"But in the end, the whole thing was a disappointment," he said. "Even after more than fifty missions over China, being fired upon by MiG fighters—well, let's just say there was no hero's welcome for us when we returned."

Darby edged a little closer and glanced into one of Gramps's scrapbooks. "I guess the war in Korea maybe didn't seem as important as the Second World War?"

He shifted his shoulders. "War isn't a popularity contest, kiddo. In the end, it was the men I fought with I cared about the most. They were the ones who put their lives on the line."

Gramps ended up telling Darby stories all afternoon, pointing out guys in his scrapbook, and showing her where he flew his missions on a map he had tucked in the back. He didn't give any sign that he knew she'd ever seen the scrapbooks before.

Nan's voice finally called through the kitchen window

to tell them dinner was ready, so Darby crawled out of their spot under the bushes. She had to help Gramps up. Sitting under the raspberry bushes had made him pretty stiff and he really hobbled on his way over to the back door. He paused, and Darby could see him stop to stretch his back out a bit. She was right behind him with the empty glasses in one hand and his scrapbook under her arm.

"Thanks for telling me about that stuff, Gramps. It's so cool you were a pilot. Wait 'til I tell my friends at school."

He looked at Darby in a puzzled way. "You never made it to school, Allie. What are you talking about?" He walked into the house and refused to say another word for the rest of the evening.

—〰—

Later that night, she was up in her room writing down a few notes in her summer journal when there was a knock at Darby's door. Nan stuck her head through the opening and smiled.

"I thought I might find you playing on your new contraption," she said, as she came in and closed the door.

Darby laughed, but she closed her journal in a hurry. "I haven't managed to play on it since that first night, Nan. Too busy, I guess."

Nan perched on the edge of the bed. "I see you are making good use of Michael Stevens's basket," she said. It was sitting on the bedside table. "That's quite a collection."

"It is, isn't it?" Darby agreed. The smooth piece of the hearthstone from the *Elizabeth* nestled in the basket, alongside the other rocks.

"You have chosen such beautiful colours," she said. "Look how striking they look together. That pale green piece against the red sandstone. Even the broken grey shard looks beautiful in that basket." She patted Darby's hand gently. "But I didn't come up here to talk about your rock collection. I just want to thank you. It was very kind of you to spend the afternoon with Gramps, dear."

"Actually, Nan, it was okay. He was telling me all about being a pilot and patrolling over China during the Korean War. I had no idea there even *was* a Korean War. At school we've only learned about the First and Second World Wars."

"Oh, your grandfather can really go on with his war stories. I remember he cut a very dashing figure in his uniform when he returned from his tour of duty."

Darby grinned. "Swept you off your feet, right, Nan?"

She smiled and smoothed a wrinkle in her dress. "Well, yes, he did. I had a very romantic vision of life in those days. Things were so different than they are now, of course. Your Gramps just wanted to take care of me and our family." Her voice faltered a little and she took on the same sort of faraway look that Darby had seen in Gramps's eyes that afternoon.

"One day, before he left for the Far East, he found me reading poetry in the graveyard." She paused and her distant look changed to a positively evil grin. "Of course, I had my sister watching for him all along, so she signalled me when he was coming and I draped myself most becomingly over an old tombstone."

Darby grinned again. "Nan! You were trying to catch yourself a boyfriend."

She blinked her eyes at her granddaughter. "Gramps hasn't figured it out to this day," she said with a straight face. They both burst out laughing.

Nan stood up and put her hand on the door. "I do want to thank you again, Darby. And I realized today that you have not been to the beach even once on this visit. I'm going to arrange a trip soon, I promise. We have to visit the shore before your parents arrive—they will be here next week!"

"Oh—okay, Nan. Thanks." A trip to the beach was the last thing on her mind. She needed to find Gabe and ask him about the *Elizabeth*.

But Nan didn't seem to notice the obvious lack of enthusiasm.

"Wonderful. It will do us all good. You certainly can't come to the Island and not even visit the beach." She looked thoughtful. "You know, Gramps is not himself these days. A trip to the shore will cheer him up, too. I think he's a bit lonely, though he doesn't seem to want to go visit with his old cronies the way he used to. There are so few of them left, I guess."

"What about Ernie, the cab driver?" Darby asked.

"Yes, Ernie is a dear. He's almost ten years younger than Vern, though, and his only experience in the war was as a supply clerk, though you'd never know it to talk to him." She smiled gently and opened the door.

"When we got married, Darby, Vernon promised to look after me, and I him. He has cared for our family all these years and I plan to do the same for him as long as I can. Thank you for helping me do that this summer."

She closed the door softly and left Darby to her thoughts.

The next morning, Gramps used up the last of the milk making his porridge, so he handed Darby enough money for milk and a pack of red licorice and sent her off to the corner store. Darby took the opportunity to skate past Gabe's house before heading to the store, but there was no sign of anyone around, and all the windows were dark.

By the time she glided back down the street with the milk under one arm, she noticed a strange car parked in front of Nan and Gramps's house. She set down her skateboard quietly on the porch and walked around the back to put the milk away in the kitchen. Nan was sitting at the kitchen table talking with a lady Darby didn't recognize.

"This is Ms. Fraser from the social services department," Nan said, her voice sounding artificially bright. "Darby is our granddaughter, from Toronto."

"Ah—from away, are you?" Ms. Fraser said with a smile. "I'm actually just leaving, but it is nice to meet you all the same." She turned to Nan.

"Thank you so much for the tea, Mrs. Christopher.

I'm glad to see you have things so under control. You'll let me know if anything changes or if you need a helping hand, won't you? I'm just a phone call away!"

She wiggled her fingers at Darby and Nan ushered her out the front door.

Darby poured herself a glass of milk and sat down at the table. Nan came in and marched over to the cookie jar, dropped two snickerdoodles on a plate and set it in front of her granddaughter.

"That woman was so irritating," she said, yanking a chair into place, and then in a high, sing-song voice: "I'm just a phone call away!"

"Nan!" Darby laughed. "Are you making fun of that poor lady?"

Nan arched her eyebrow. "Oh, the woman means well, I'm sure. She's only doing her job. It seems the Charlottetown Fire Department filed a report with senior social services when they had to help Gramps out of the tree that time. They wanted to make sure that Gramps was not 'out of control,' as she so delicately put it."

"Sheesh, Nan—that was more than a month ago."

"I know. Ms. Fraser is proof that even good intentions move slowly when a civil servant is involved. But I told her that Gramps is just fine. He is under Dr. Brian's care and there is nothing to worry about."

"A civil servant? Does that mean she works for servant's wages?"

Nan laughed. "Not these days, my dear. It just means she works for one of the levels of government. My guess is it's the busy-body level."

Nan bustled out of the room to relieve her frustrations by cleaning the bathroom and Darby stayed at the table, finishing her cookies and thinking. Spying Gramps on the back porch, she went out to offer him the last snickerdoodle. He was looking for his glasses.

Darby had spent a lot of time on this visit looking for Gramps's glasses, mostly because Gramps's idea of looking for something was bawling "Etta!" and grumbling until the item was found. Gramps had several pairs of glasses. Most of them were the fifteen-dollar drugstore variety with magnifying lenses and spectacularly ugly frames. But he also had a pair of regular glasses that didn't look quite as dorky as the others, and of course those were the ones that got lost.

For some reason that morning, Nan was extra upset by the loss of the glasses. "He's just getting more scatterbrained by the day," she whispered to Darby.

Darby blamed Ms. Fraser's visit, of course. She had freaked Nan out.

"Anybody can lose a pair of glasses, Nan. My dad loses his all the time. We usually find them on his head."

Nan didn't feel better until the glasses were actually found. They turned up on top of the fridge. When Darby pulled them down, Nan suddenly remembered that she had put them up there when she was bleaching the sink after Ms. Fraser's visit.

Of course, this made Gramps very happy, but it left Nan more worried than ever. What if *her* memory was going, too?

Darby shook her head and went to gather her swimsuit

and towel. Quite clearly, she was not the first and only
Dark-side Darby.

Worries aside, Nan's beach trip was all arranged, and
so that afternoon they headed out, safely deposited by
Ernie at a beach that Gramps chose himself.

Darby stuck a toe in the water and it was pretty chilly.
Still, looking around, she decided Gramps was right—this
was a good choice for a beach. It was near Stanhope,
which is one of the most popular beaches on the north
shore of the Island, but even in the middle of a hot
August afternoon, there was almost nobody around.

They'd climbed from the parking lot, over boardwalks
built to protect the sand dunes and down to the beach.
The sand stretched out, flat and rusty red as far as Darby
could see in both directions. Way down at the end, she
could just spy the very top of an old lighthouse. Off shore,
a little a fishing boat bobbed gently at its moorings. For
the first two hours, the only other visitors had been a single other family, sitting a good distance down the beach.

"I hate the dunes," Gramps grumbled. "Too much
sand in my shoes."

"The dunes are protected now, Vern," Nan said, adjust-
ing her giant sun hat. "You're not supposed to step off the
boardwalks. Besides, this spot is perfect. The sand is flat
and it won't get into your shoes at all. Now just help yourself to a drink out of that cooler and enjoy the day."

Darby felt a rush of sympathy for Gramps on this
one. But Nan had the firm belief that a person can't visit
PEI and not go to the beach. So when she arranged for
Ernie to drive the family on his afternoon off from being

a cabbie, what was a girl to do? Agreeing with a big fake smile on her face was the only option. Gramps contributed by suggesting a location he remembered from who knows when, and grumbling about every part of the day. Darby wanted to join him, but Nan had gone to a lot of trouble. And after Ms. Fraser's visit, Darby didn't want to add to Nan's problems.

The truth was, though, at home in Toronto, Darby was generally more of a pool girl. There were a couple of pretty decent swimming pools in the area and that's really as close to the beach as she was ever interested in getting. But the afternoon wasn't going too badly, and she had high hopes that Gramps would only last an hour or so more under the sun before he demanded to go home. Then maybe Darby would have a few minutes to chase down Gabe after all.

She turned back to her reading. She'd brought a couple of library books and Nan had even supplied an ancient beach chair to sit on. Looking at the pile beside her, Darby decided the total number of books she had read in her life was easily doubled by the reading she had done over the summer. Every librarian in the downtown branch knew her by name.

Nan had Gramps put up an umbrella and the two of them sat underneath it with the odd, excellent posture of old folks. Darby had just managed to plunge back into the smallpox rosters from the quarantine stations on Grosse-Île when family-style trouble arrived in the form of a woman with three little kids.

With the whole beach stretched out empty before them, Darby expected the family to pick a nice, open place to spread out. Instead, they set up right in front of Gramps's umbrella, the kids dumping a huge pile of plastic buckets and toys practically on Darby's feet and then proceeding to fight over them.

Gramps looked over at Darby and rolled his eyes. *Compadrés in beach torture,* she thought, and smiled back at him.

"Why don't you try having a quick swim, dear?" Nan suggested. Darby jumped up, thinking a swim might be just the thing to speed them all out of there.

The woman plopped her fat baby boy on the sand. "April!" she called. "Juniper! Let's build a sand castle, girls."

Darby could see Gramps examining his shoes as the sand sprayed over him. She carefully set the library books out of harm's way and ran into the low waves lapping the shore.

The water temperature was pretty cool, but once she was in it was okay. Darby kept a wary eye out for jellyfish. Those little purple blobs she'd seen in the ocean seemed a lot bigger when a person was actually in the water with them. She tried a regular front crawl stroke to begin with, but the strong taste of salt water in her mouth soon had her switching over to the old head-above-the-water flail. She decided a ten-minute dip would cover her in Nan's eyes, and it was likely Gramps would be nothing but grateful. Ernie was due back soon, anyway, so Darby hoped the trip wouldn't last too much longer.

Unfortunately, as soon as she hit the water, both of the little girls from the proximity-challenged family on the beach decided to jump in as well. While the mother scrambled to put a life jacket on one of them, the other one was screaming to get in. Darby paddled farther out and was floating on her back for a minute, mostly to keep her ears under water to cut some of the noise, when she noticed a sudden flurry of activity in the water.

She was out deep enough that her feet couldn't quite touch the bottom, so she tried to remember how to tread water while she figured out what was going on. It took a minute to coordinate her legs and arms, but once she had it nailed she glanced over toward the beach. Nan's umbrella was flying through the air. This was so strange, Darby stopped treading and flailed her way closer to try to find a spot where she might actually be able to put her feet down.

A second or two later a sandbar rose up under the water. Darby dug her toes in and pulled herself over to where it was shallow enough to stand. She had actually floated quite a way out, so when she looked back it took a few seconds to see what was happening at that distance. She could see Nan standing beside the upturned umbrella, but she was making no attempt to set it upright. In fact, Nan started running toward the shore. Where was Gramps?

Darby suddenly spotted a white head bobbing in the waves. She dove off the sandbar and, salty mouth or not, did her best front crawl toward him.

All she could think was *Gramps can't swim, Gramps can't swim.* But in the minute or two it took her to get back to the beach, everyone was safely back on shore again. Another strike against Dark-side Darby, worrying about nothing, as usual.

Darby staggered out of the water to find the mother holding one of her screaming kids and running at Gramps, who was pulling the other one, kicking and also screaming, out of the water.

Nan was standing at the shoreline, and Darby could hear Gramps calling to her. "I've got her, Etta—she's all right, don't worry about a thing."

The mother looked relieved as she reached for the child from Gramps's arms. "Thank you so much, sir. I think she would have been fine, but I was so busy getting the jacket on April, I didn't see her run in."

But Gramps pulled the kid away from the mother with a kind smile, and turned to Nan. "Here's Allie, Etta. I told you she'd be fine. I brought her back to you, just like I promised."

Nan was gesturing wildly at Gramps, trying to get him to hand the child back to her mother. Her face was very red and she looked close to tears. "This little girl is called Juniper, Vern. She belongs to this lady. Please hand her back to her mother."

Gramps looked puzzled, and by that time the lady was nervous enough to snatch the little girl out of his hands.

In the few seconds it took Darby to try to understand what was going on, something happened to time. She couldn't explain it, any more than she would ever be able to tell her new teacher how she spent her summer holidays. Thinking about it afterwards, Darby realized it was probably just in her mind. But at the time it was like one of those dreams where she'd suddenly lost her ability to run and everything goes into slow motion. Like that, except a million times worse.

Darby heard the mother say, "Come along, April, let's move our things down the beach," and she had time to feel resentful about how clueless she was about Gramps's good intentions. Darby bent to grab her towel and try to straighten up the umbrella. Behind her, Nan had walked over, put her hand on the woman's arm and was whispering something apologetically. Darby caught sight of Ernie coming across the beach and had time to wonder why he had broken into a run when she turned to see Gramps fall like a log—straight forward into the ocean.

Ernie, Nan and Darby all got to Gramps at the same time, and Ernie turned him over and pulled his face out of the water.

Gramps's skin was pale; his lips so white they were almost blue. He gasped like a fish, just once. "Allie is safe now, Etta," he said, but he didn't look at Nan. He didn't look at anyone. All at once, he just wasn't there anymore.

And time started up again.

Ernie tossed Darby his cell phone. "Just push the button with the red letter 'E,' kid," he said, grunting a little as he pulled Gramps further out of the water. "It'll go straight through to the ambulance."

Ernie dropped down on his knees in the wet sand and started giving Gramps CPR. He stopped only to tell Darby the directions to relay to the ambulance crew. The woman with the children stood off to one side, trying to hold her baby and keep the two girls away. In the end,

Nan took one of the little girls in her own arms when the kid mistook what was happening for a game and tried to jump on Gramps's legs. It was sickening, but Nan stayed completely calm.

By the time Darby snapped the cell phone shut, she could hear the sirens in the distance. She ran to get the paramedics from the parking lot, and they came flying behind her back across the boardwalk and then the sand, carrying a portable canvas stretcher.

Ernie didn't stop trying to help Gramps breathe until one of the paramedics actually pulled him off.

Where's Gabe? Darby thought wildly. As if he could do anything. Not even the paramedics could help, no matter how hard they tried. Gramps was gone.

Nan followed the paramedics over the dunes to the ambulance, and they watched Gramps get loaded onto a proper stretcher inside. One of the paramedics then helped Nan into the back.

"You ride with me, Darby," Ernie said. He had somehow managed to hoist all the gear up and was standing in the parking lot beside the ambulance. When Darby looked at him, she saw he had a bit of sand stuck to his face, beside his mouth.

The doors slammed closed on the ambulance.

"Ernie," Darby grabbed his arm. "Who is Allie?"

"You'd best talk to your Nan about that, dear," he said and threw all their beach gear into his trunk.

Darby sat on the front porch with Nan that night, as she told the story of her little girl, lost—drowned—before she was even two years old. The child had been named Alice after her great-grandmother, but Vernon Christopher had taken one look at his baby girl and she had been Allie from that moment on. She was the apple of her daddy's eye, and he spent every minute he was away from work with her.

"One afternoon, your gramps offered to take her for a while so I could have a nap," Nan said. "You know your dad's birthday is in September? Well, he was about a month away from being born. It was a hot day, just like this one, and Gramps took her to a park not too far from here."

"The one just down Forsyth Street?" Darby asked.

Nan shook her head. Her eyes were red and she clutched a tissue in one hand, but Darby hadn't seen her cry a single tear. "No. The park was closer to the other side of town where we lived in those days. It's gone now."

She paused for a minute.

"You don't have to tell me now," Darby said. "This has been such a hard day."

Nan reached over and hugged her granddaughter tightly. "I am so sorry for that, love."

"Nan! Please don't say sorry. Nothing that happened today was your fault."

Nan looked at Darby closely. "I haven't heard Vern mention Allie's name in more than thirty years," she said, and smiled a little. "This summer was supposed to be a lovely holiday for you and a break for your parents," she said softly. "And instead, I am the one who had the best time, because it has given me the chance to get to know you."

"I'm glad I came," Darby said. "I've learned a lot, too."

"It was just a little nap, in the end," she said, and for a minute Darby thought she was talking about herself, all those years ago. "He dozed off on the bench at the park. She climbed out of her pram and ended up in the wading pool."

"Oh, Nan." Darby didn't know what to say.

"He never spoke her name again until today." Nan closed her eyes and leaned her head onto the porch railing.

Darby didn't say a word.

After that, Nan told Darby some things she already knew, or guessed. That Nan and Gramps had gone on to have three boys. And that the boys grew up knowing they had once had an older sister, but no details had ever been discussed. She told Darby how, for reasons she never understood, Gramps was always hardest on Darby's dad, the first boy born after the loss of his only girl.

Late that night, when everyone had gone, Darby lay awake and listened to her grandmother weep at last, over her own loss—the man she had loved for more than fifty years.

Chapter Thirteen

The sound of the doorbell woke Darby the next morning. It might as well have been a starter's pistol. A steady stream of women poured in, each overflowing with kindness and ready to help.

Darby decided this was a good thing. Ladies sat with Nan and made lists and telephone calls, and pot after pot after pot of hot tea.

She had at least five different women offer to make her breakfast. After refusing for what felt like the fiftieth time, Darby grabbed a banana and escaped to the back porch.

With the door closed, all she could hear was the hum of a bee in what was left of the raspberries. All the bustle was a good thing for Nan. Her friends had closed ranks, her sisters were organizing everyone and everything, and in the little Darby had seen of her, she seemed back to the old Nan. Not a tissue or a red eye in sight.

But all the bustle was too much for Darby. She wasn't hungry, but she couldn't remember ever longing more for the taste of porridge in her life.

She left the skateboard on the front porch for once. It wasn't worth having to walk past Nan's honour guard. She cut through the hedge in the yard and walked down the lane that came out at the back of Gabe's place. There was a spot where the hedge parted at one end, and she pushed through and into the secret garden.

Gabe was nowhere in sight. Maybe he was gone for good. Darby's parents were due to arrive tomorrow, and then there would be the funeral. And after that, they would take her home.

Strange how it didn't feel so much like home anymore.

She looked up at the blue house. Nan had said it had been a different colour when Gramps was born here. And now he was dead.

Darby suddenly realized that if just a couple of things had been different, she might never have met her Gramps. If her mom and dad hadn't dumped her in Charlottetown. If they'd changed their minds about the reno. If she'd spent the summer skateboarding in Toronto, like she'd planned.

For a few more hours, at least, this was still her secret garden. Her grandfather had been born in this house. Her dad had stolen apples here.

And Darby? She hopped up the stone windowsill.

She'd had a few adventures of her own.

This time Darby knew right away it was a boat— maybe the trip on the coffin ship had given her sea legs. When she got her bearings, Darby found herself in much nicer quarters than probably existed on the *Elizabeth*. It was a small room with space for only two low beds and a tiny writing desk with a stack of books on the floor beside it. At the bottom of each bed was a good-sized trunk. One of the beds looked recently slept in. The other was tidily made up.

The door was closed tightly but not locked. Darby didn't dare sit down on the beds in case one of the room's occupants showed up and sat on her, so she used the pile of books by the desk as a little stool and sat down to wait.

It wasn't long before the door flung open. The room was so small that the door couldn't swing freely; it hit one of the beds and bounced back.

"Careful—careful with the door." The person speaking backed into the room, carrying one end of something that looked pretty heavy.

"A moment, please, Alasdair," came the other voice. "I do not care to slip."

Alasdair grunted, and Darby could see he was carrying one end of a very large wooden crate. The thing was so big it was giving him trouble as he tried to steer it through the small doorway. "Just a little—further—to—the—right—" he said, and then the box was in and Gabe was there, too, beaming at Darby and closing the door behind him.

"Nice room you have here," he said.

Alasdair raised an eyebrow. "Very funny, young Monroe. You know, when I agreed to supervise your passage to the colonies, it did not occur to me to enquire of your father whether you had the strength of character to properly make up your bed each day."

"Each day," cried Gabriel, in mock surprise and with a wicked Scottish accent. "I had no idea your standards would be so stringent." He plopped down on his unmade bed. "At least I earn my keep through brawn."

"Yes, I do thank you for your help with this behemoth," Alasdair said. "I have no faith those laggards down in the holds will treat it with the care it requires, so I mean to bring it ashore myself when we disembark later today."

"Yourself?" It was Gabe's turn to look sceptical. "It seems I may still be of use to you right to the end, then."

"Indeed," said Alasdair. The lid of the chest at the bottom of his bed creaked as he lifted it. From inside he pulled out a small crowbar. "I'll just have a quick peek to check that all is well," he added.

Gabe laughed. "I don't believe you for a moment," he said. "You know very well that nothing has shifted inside the crate. You just want to look at your prize again."

Alasdair managed to pry up one corner of the lid. He grinned at Gabe. "Perhaps. But would you care to take a glance?"

Darby craned over to look, too. Inside the crate was a series of metal cylinders, each carefully numbered and nestled into thick rolls of paper cushioning.

Gabe gazed at the contents of the crate. "You mean to tell me with all that weight, the press is not even assembled inside?"

Alasdair picked up one of the cylinders and examined it critically. "We certainly could never lift it if it were," he said. "When assembled, it will weigh many hundreds of pounds. But I was concerned that these cylinders were particularly fragile, so I assured myself of their care by wrapping them up individually for the journey."

He sat back down on the bed, the cylinder still in his hand.

"These new presses have hundreds of moving parts," he said. "I have been using a rotary press to print my newspaper in Inverness for several years, but this is a new design, envisioned by an American named Bullock." He held up the cylinder. "When assembled, this small piece will help to automatically feed the paper through the rollers. No more hand feeding! It will mean a tremendous jump in productivity."

"I have heard of William Bullock," said Gabe. "But I thought he invented farm tools."

Alasdair took the cylinder and carefully replaced it in its wrapping. "Yes, yes," he said impatiently, as if the subject didn't really interest him. "But it is his work with printing presses that will mean the biggest opportunity for me." He sat back on the tiny part of his bed that was not covered in wooden crate. "This press will be self-adjusting, will print on both sides and fold the paper before cutting it. If my father's research holds true, it will be the first of its kind in the Canadas."

"And what will that mean for you?" asked Gabe.

"It means I will, in fact, be able to make a living here, I hope," said Alasdair. "My father does not share my late mother's low opinion of this small island, God rest her, and he has long established himself as a permanent resident. He has offered me part of the capital I require to take this step."

Gabe pointed to a small box nestled in the top of Alasdair's trunk. "Does that contain more pieces of your precious press?"

Alasdair picked up the small box and opened the lid. "'Tis nothing," he said briefly. "Merely a small token for my father—and little more than a maudlin reminder of the country of my birth, in truth." He tilted the box to show that it held a scoop of rich brown Scottish soil, mixed with a few rocks and pebbles. "He asked me to bring a piece of Scotland with me that he might plant it in the earth. Just more weight to carry, as far as I am concerned."

He closed the lid of the trunk and set the box carelessly on the top. "I do believe I shall have a quick look into the hold, just to ensure the rest of the press is in good shape after the voyage."

He glanced over at Gabe, lying with his hands behind his head in comfort. "I'll expect to see that bed in proper shape, young man," he said sternly. "I want to be able to give your family a good report when I put you into their hands this afternoon."

The door closed behind him and Darby jumped up. She wanted to hug Gabe, she was so happy to see him, but there wasn't really room to get around the big crate, so she contented herself with grinning at him like an idiot.

"Where have you been?" she asked.

He hopped up and started making his bed. "I have been around," he said. He punched a pillow into place and looked at Darby gravely. "I am sorry for the loss of your grandfather."

Darby nodded. Her heart seemed too full, suddenly, to even ask how Gabe knew what had happened. "I feel pretty grateful I had the chance to get to know him a little before he was gone."

Gabe opened the door and stepped out of the room, leaving it slightly ajar. His eyes twinkled a little over his shoulder. "Perhaps you will get to know a little more, even now. This journey will be brief, Darby. Let us take the opportunity to look about us a little. You must learn while you can."

It was a foggy day when Darby followed Gabe onto the narrow deck that circled the ship outside the staterooms. Outside of Alasdair's room the sky was pearly grey, and it looked ready to rain. She leaned against the deck rail and watched as the ship glided slowly toward a small port town. Several wooden wharves poked out into the water. She could see that the harbour was well protected and there was a lot of action on the docks as preparations were made for the landing. The ship bumped gently against the quay, and bumped again, before ropes were thrown to tie it in place.

"This vessel was built on the Island a few years ago," said Alasdair, who came striding up a nearby staircase, taking the steps three at a time with his long legs. "One of the crewmen just told me that after they leave here, they will ship out for New Zealand."

"Now, that is a long journey," said Gabe, looking at the activity on the docks. "I wonder if my family is here yet."

Alasdair looked out over the harbour. "Seems a civil enough place," he muttered under his breath. He glanced at Gabe and then unfolded a letter from his pocket. "My father's farm is north of Charlottetown, but according to his last letter, he will make the trip down to arrive late this evening. I believe we will stay here overnight before heading back to meet my brothers. He says your family will be waiting to meet you here, also."

Gabe nodded. "How has he taken the news of the loss of your mother?" he asked quietly.

Alasdair sighed and stared off into the bustling town. "My father lost my mother the day they first laid eyes on this very harbour," he said, and his voice held a deep note of pain. "I was very small and remember almost nothing at all about the crossing. In those days, my family had very little in the way of capital and it had taken nearly all they had to make the trip from Inverness. But my mother was shaken with horror at the sight of Prince Edward Island. I believe a few of the Mi'kmaq elders arrived to meet the ship and the sight of native people truly frightened her."

Gabe raised his eyebrows. "They should have been more frightened of us," he said. "The new settlers changed the lives of the native peoples around here forever."

"Killed many of them, too," Alasdair added. "The diseases settlers have brought to the area have devastated many of the native populations. I have covered this extensively in my newspaper, and hope to do more of that when I get established here. And this also played a large part in the worries of my mother."

Gabe leaned on the rail. "Your mother was afraid this place was a haven for disease?"

"Well, we travelled on a decent ship, of course," Alasdair said. "But it was a scant year after the typhus epidemic had spread through the colonies, and initially upon our arrival she refused to see the quarantine doctor." He sighed. "I do not know what happened after that. I remember only that she set her lips in a tight line, sat herself down on her trunk and refused to move. And when the ship had its return sailing, my mother sailed with it, along with my youngest brother and sister. And myself, of course."

Below, Darby could see where the ship's crew was working with the men on the dock, struggling to place an enormous gangplank.

"What made you decide to come back to Charlottetown?" asked Gabe.

Alasdair shrugged. "All my family is here now,"
he said. "My sister and brother came across years ago,
but I had a thriving newspaper business in Inverness
and mother to care for, of course." He laughed bitterly. "I was engaged to be married, but the young
woman saw fit to turn her attentions elsewhere and
so, when my mother died . . ."

"You decided to come."

Alasdair nodded, his attention on the unloading
going on down below. "Hey!" he cried suddenly.
"Avast! Ahoy!" He turned to Gabe. "Blast, I think they
have just dropped one of the press boxes. Can you
accompany me, lad?"

Gabe shot a grin at Darby and hurried off after
Alasdair as he flew down the stairwell.

She leaned against the ship's railing and watched
as things unfolded below. Some of the passengers had
begun to disembark from another gangway, and Darby
could see a meandering line heading toward a building with a sign marked Immigration.

The greyness above started to break a little, and
a ray of sun shone through the cracks in the clouds.
Tiny sparkles danced on the waves that lapped up
against the heavy lumber of the docks below. She
wondered about Alasdair's mother, so fearful of this
new land. The shoreline of Charlottetown looked
markedly different from her own experience, with
many more trees and fewer buildings. Twenty-five
years before this time, it must have looked more
worrisome still, with vast areas of uncleared forest.

But was it worth the loss of a marriage and the breakup of a family?

Darby felt a knot tighten in her stomach. Would her own family break up the same way? She had heard nothing of this from her parents, of course, but maybe they had just been shielding her from the worst over the summer.

Her attention was drawn to Alasdair and Gabe as they appeared on the dock below, but the stevedores clearly weren't happy having two uppity passengers do their jobs for them. Finally, they seemed content to settle on waving Gabe's efforts away entirely and allowing Alasdair to walk alongside as his precious boxes were loaded onto the Charlottetown quay.

The sun was well and truly out now and steam began to rise from the wet surfaces around the dockyard. A number of wagons and buggies were pulled up along the street, with people hurrying to meet their arriving relatives. Darby wondered idly why the window had brought her here—to this place and this time. Was it to see Charlottetown as others saw it, near its beginnings?

She looked down again to see Gabe waving. Darby waved back and nodded when he gestured for her to join him.

A family, well laden with possessions from their stateroom, were slowly making their way down the stairs. The mother had her hands full, literally, trying to keep track of a small boy and carry a number of items.

She walked beside what must be her teenaged son and daughter, also heavily loaded with bags and boxes. Darby slipped in behind, and followed them down.

The little boy, no more than four or five, was filled with excited questions. "Will there be Red Indians, Mama? Or Chinamen? Andrew told me the colonies are full of strange people from everywhere under the sun."

His mother shifted her load and squeezed his hand. "Andrew should not be telling his young brother tall tales to frighten him," she said severely, clearly talking to the older boy who was almost invisible under an enormous pile of boxes.

"Well, it *is* true, Mama," the older boy looked back at them over his shoulder. "Papa has said as much in his letters, and I have learned more at school. We may have come from Scotland, but others have emigrated from France and China and even England."

Darby had to stifle a laugh at this one, wondering if the English were as exotic to the little boy as the other peoples he would meet in his new country.

The girl walking beside Andrew sniffed. "You mustn't call them the colonies anymore, Simon," she said to her little brother. "The colonies all joined together and became the Dominion of Canada several years ago."

"You don't know everything, Lizzie," said Andrew, obviously trying to redeem himself in his mother's eyes. "Prince Edward Island didn't agree to join the confederation until last year. And since British Columbia joined in 1871, there is talk of the Northwest Territories being split up into provinces and taking part as well."

They stepped onto the gangplank and a crew member rushed forward to help with their bags. Simon's mother scooped him up in her arms. "Well, whoever lives here and wherever they came from, your papa says it is the land of the future. And now it will be our home."

"Take a deep breath, Simon," said his brother. "This is what your new home smells like."

"I smell green apples," said Lizzie. "Does anyone else smell apples?"

Darby hurriedly stepped back a little and tucked her hair behind her ears.

"Look!" shouted Andrew. "There's Papa!"

The children ran toward a smiling man who stood in the doorway of the immigration shed and Darby took her too-recently shampooed self over to where Gabe was standing.

"Do I smell of apples to you?" she hissed at him.

He shrugged. "All I can smell is the docks—and perhaps cinnamon," he said, as a man bearing a large spice-laden crate trundled by.

"They shipped cinnamon from Scotland?" Darby asked, staring after the man with the crate.

"Perhaps not from Scotland, but through Scottish ports," Gabe said. "The ports were the gateways to the world."

A voice called "Fergus!" and Gabe's head snapped to look.

"Fergus?" Darby muttered. "I thought you were called Monroe."

"Ach, I have many names," he said with a smile. He lifted a hand to wave at Alasdair, now standing with an elderly gentleman.

It was Gramps.

Darby felt her legs go weak.

Alasdair waved Gabe over. "Father, may I present my young travelling companion, Fergus Monroe. Fergus, my father, Allan Urquhart."

Gabe-known-as-Fergus caught Darby's eye as he shook Alasdair's father's hand. He actually winked at her. All she could do was gape in shock.

"Fergus." Urquhart gravely bowed.

Darby knew it wasn't Gramps as soon as she heard the highland burr, softened but not lost after nearly twenty years away from Scotland. But the resemblance was unbelievable—a face for the ages. Allan Urquhart, her grandfather's great-grandfather. And the answer to her question. This was why she found herself in Charlottetown in 1875. No crisis to witness, no horror to remember. Just the last piece of her own family puzzle, snapped into place.

Alasdair slipped something into Gabe's hand and slapped him on the back.

Gabe bowed slightly to Allan Urquhart and then stepped off to one side as father and son began the slow process of getting to know each other again.

Darby slid back into the shadow of the building so that Gabe would be able to speak with her unobserved.

"I must go," he said quietly, turning his back to the flurry of activity on the dock.

"I know," she said. "Alasdair said he would take you to your family."

Gabe pointed to a tiny stone building at the end of one of the wharves. "Your route home is through that doorway," he said.

Darby clutched at his arm as he turned to go. "Gabe—you know I am leaving in a couple of days."

"I knew it would be very soon," he said, and his smile left him for a moment. "I *am* terribly sorry about your grandfather," he added softly. "I hope these small journeys helped you find something of what you seek."

Darby didn't know what to say.

"But wait," he said, and his face lit up again. "I nearly forgot."

He reached in his pocket. "For your collection," he said. "From Alasdair. His father was thrilled to see the highland soil, but said he had ploughed enough rocks to last a lifetime."

He pressed the stone into Darby's hand. For the first time in all her summer's travels, she held something warm. It was a small rock, flat, grey and almost heart-shaped. "From the heart of the highlands to the heart of Canada," he whispered.

She had to laugh. "I thought I told you that Toronto was the heart of Canada."

"That you must decide for yourself," he replied, and as he stepped away from her, his eyes gleamed. "See you around, sometime," he said. Without another word, he turned and followed Alasdair and his father through the door of the immigration shed.

"See you," Darby whispered.

It was time to go home.

Chapter Fourteen

Death by misadventure.

Misadventure.

That's what a coroner calls it when a grand-father runs into the water to save a toddler. Even when the toddler doesn't need saving, not really. And even when the toddler is not the toddler he thinks he's saving. One that he didn't manage to save nearly fifty years before.

Darby sat in the funeral parlour and thought about the coroner. Who would want that job? Looking at dead bodies and trying to figure out how they got that way. The PEI coroner told Nan that Gramps's heart attack was probably brought on by the rescue of the little girl. He also told her that Gramps's brain showed evidence of Alzheimer's.

Darby tried not to think about what Gramps looked like when Ernie pulled him out of the water. She'd seen so much death already this summer—why should his be any different?

He was Gramps. That made it different.

The night before, when she had run home from Gabe's house, she'd got to the top of the stairs by her room before she realized she didn't have a headache. No aura. Not even a trace of pain.

Just a rock in her pocket, still warm from the hands of the man who brought his family—her family—to Canada.

The sign over the door said Viewing Room, but Darby was alone with Gramps and there wasn't any viewing going on. His casket was not much more than a plain wooden box with some kind of brass handles. Not too shiny.

Darby figured the least she could do was to sit with him. Her parents weren't set to arrive until later. Besides, Gramps had agreed to take her to the beach. Mostly because Nan had talked him into it, but still. His last trip away from his house was because of Darby. She couldn't take this trip with him, of course, but she could at least sit with him a while.

Nan came into the room. Every time Darby had seen her since Gramps had died, she had been surrounded by women. Darby had recognized some of them: the two sisters she had first met that day in the front yard with the fire department; and there were Shawnie, and Fiona; Dr. Brian's wife, Addie, had been over, too. Darby didn't have a clue who most of the others were.

But for once, Nan wasn't surrounded by all the clucking old hens. She sat down beside Darby with a sigh, and took her hand.

"I was wondering where you'd gotten to," she said in a low voice.

"It didn't seem like you really needed any help," Darby said. "So I thought I'd just sit here a while."

"Ernie is here. He wants to take you to the airport to meet your parents."

Darby stood up reluctantly. She wasn't at all sure she was ready to face her parental units so soon. "Okay. Is there anything you would like me to do first, Nan?"

Nan shook her head. "No, I think everything is looked after. The service is this afternoon, and—" She sat quietly for a moment, then stood to take Darby's face in her hands. "Oh, I am so going to miss you, girlie, when you go back home. I have become accustomed to having you here. The house will feel so empty with you gone."

"With both of us gone," Darby said, bitterly. "Nan, this is all my fault. If you and Gramps hadn't had to drag me to the beach that day, he would still be here with you."

Nan dropped her hands to Darby's shoulders and gave her granddaughter a little shake. "Don't you even think such a thing," she said severely. "In the first place, the trip to the beach that day was my idea. And," she sighed a little, "if it comes right down to it, your Gramps was already almost gone. Any hope I had of trying to care for him in our home was lost."

She smiled sadly. "After he burned his uniform with the iron, well, I should have seen how serious things were."

The door opened and Ernie poked his head in. "Ready to go to the airport, Miss Darby?" he said with a gentle smile. "Oh, and you can come, too, kid."

Nan arched an eyebrow. "Very funny," she said, dryly.

"I think I'll just go home and get changed, if you don't mind, dear," she added, looking at Darby. "You bring your mother and dad right into the house when you get back."

They followed the still-chuckling Ernie out the door.

—⚏—

The funeral was held at Trinity United Church that afternoon. Darby was surprised at how many people packed the benches inside. *I guess a person makes a few friends over a life that long,* she thought.

She was not as surprised, however, as she had been at the airport when her mother walked into the arrivals section. Darby's mother had beamed at her, yelled "Surprise!" and given her daughter a huge hug. Literally huge, seeing as her mother was at least twenty pounds heavier than when she had kissed her goodbye in Toronto. And Darby was pretty sure it hadn't come from eating doughnuts because she was missing her only daughter.

"Honey, you're going to be a big sister!" she yelled. Just in case Darby had missed it—or any of the hundreds of other passengers in the airport had.

"Uh, congratulations," Darby said, feeling strange. Her grandfather was dead, a new baby was coming and from the beaming smiles on her parents' faces, she guessed she'd been a little off base about the whole divorce idea. She wasn't actually sure how she should feel, but for the moment she settled on feeling a little sick.

They had to go through the whole thing all over again when they walked out to Ernie's cab. He had known

Darby's dad while he was growing up, and soon the three of them were all talking at once about the baby, and the parental units' worries because of their advanced ages and the reno, which was finally done. When they got to the house, Nan got into the action, too.

Darby stood a little to one side, just listening. The strangest thing seemed to have happened to her dad's voice. It took her a few moments to figure it out, but suddenly she realized he was speaking with an Island accent. She'd never heard it in his voice before. Maybe it got stronger when he was surrounded by all the other Maritime accents. It made Darby think of Gabe, and how his voice changed depending where they travelled. And then Darby started to wonder about her own accent. She knew *she* didn't have an accent.

Did she?

———✕———

People will do whatever they can to get through a funeral. Darby didn't remember much about the service, except that a bunch of old guys from Gramps's Legion dressed up in their uniforms. Everybody had a lot of nice things to say about him. Near the end of the service, the minister invited people to share their memories of Gramps. Michael and Shawnie both got up to talk about how he helped mow their lawn. Doctor Brian got up to speak and Fiona Grady had a few nice things to say, too. Even Darby's dad managed to say a few words about his own father. He spoke quickly, with his head down, but he smiled at Darby when he was done. She hugged him tightly when he sat back down beside her, and she could feel his shoulders shake a little at this last, sudden goodbye.

Afterwards, there was a reception in the church hall and all the ladies tried to outdo themselves with fancy recipes for the sort of finger foods you usually only see in women's magazines. Everyone was laughing and milling around, and even Nan seemed to be enjoying herself.

Darby stood against a wall with a pinwheel sandwich in one hand. She quickly discovered that if her hands were empty, one of the church ladies would push more food on her, so the sandwich was running interference. Darby didn't know how all those people could eat so much. It was like they had never seen food before.

She just stood there, feeling a little queasy, until she noticed Shawnie Stevens making her way through the crowd. Darby waved the hand not holding the sandwich.

"Hi, Darby," Shawnie said quietly. "You remember my husband, Michael?"

Darby nodded at him.

"I'm very sorry for your loss," he said, in his soft voice. "I'll see you at home a bit later, Shawn," he added, and handed her a small box he had been carrying.

"Is that something for Nan?" Darby asked, wondering how they were going to find room on the table for even more food.

"No, it's actually something for you," Shawnie said, and her face flushed. "I'm a bit worried about this," she continued, her words tumbling out almost as if she was embarrassed. "When I heard what had happened, I just wanted to do something for you that might help, so I hope you're not upset with your nan and me."

Darby was totally baffled. How could she possibly be upset with Nan at a time like this?

She took the box from Shawnie and opened it. Inside was a small *inuksuk*, maybe ten inches high, like a miniature version of the one Darby had seen on her very first adventure of the summer.

"It's for your grandpa," Shawnie said softly. "To help him find his way on his journey."

Darby stared at it for a minute before she realized.

"You've used my rocks," she said, hardly believing her eyes.

"Oh, I hope you don't mind, Darby," Shawnie said, her voice filled with concern. "When your grandma told me you had been using Michael's basket for storing your favourite rocks, I thought this might be a special way to remember your grandfather."

Darby lifted the *inuksuk* out of the box and set it carefully on the table. The base was made of her round, flat piece of red PEI sandstone, and the other rocks were balanced on top. The piece of the Irish hearthstone was there and so was the heart-shaped stone from the Scottish highlands. Sitting on the base beside the *inuksuk* was the piece of soapstone.

"I carved that one a little," Shawnie said as Darby picked it up. "I really hope you don't mind."

It was a tiny green polar bear.

—⟋⟍—

After the reception, they took Gramps's ashes to be interred at the military section of the Sherwood Cemetery, and then Ernie drove the family back home in his cab. While Darby's parents were getting settled, she grabbed her skateboard and took it out onto the street. Somehow, though, she didn't feel like riding, so she propped it on the front porch and walked up to the old blue house.

The air was a little cool, and Darby tucked her knobbly knitted sweater tightly around her arms. Summer was almost over. In a day or two, she and her family were due to fly home to Toronto.

Of course, there was no sign of Gabe. Darby didn't expect to see him. Not really. A yellow piece of paper fluttered in the wind where it was stuck up near the front door. She ignored it and walked around the side of the house. One section of the back wall had caved in over the past few days—she wondered how she'd missed seeing it. Darby just stood there, staring at the house, thinking about all that had happened over one short summer.

Maybe there *was* no Gabe. That's what the rational part of her mind said. Maybe he was simply a figment of her over-active imagination.

"You'd better close that mouth of yours. You'll catch flies." She jumped a little, but it wasn't Gabe showing up to prove her wrong—or crazy.

Instead, it was Nan who smiled as she walked up. "I thought you might want this," she said, and held out the skateboard.

"Wow, thanks, Nan," Darby said. "You didn't need to carry that all the way over here for me."

"I know I didn't. But I wanted to talk with you for just a moment or two." She glanced up at the house. "Did you see the building permit out front?"

"The yellow paper?"

Nan nodded. "I was thinking about your friend who was staying here." She turned a steady gaze to the hole in the back of the house. "I guess he's not here anymore?"

Darby shook her head. "I guess not. I never really got to say goodbye, either."

"I'm sorry to hear that," she said. "But I was remembering the people who lived here when I was a young girl. They were an Acadian family. I think they eventually moved on to Tignish, or maybe somewhere in Nova Scotia."

"Acadian?" I said. "Really?"

"Yes. They were the ones who painted the house this colour blue. I think it was sort of a cream colour before, but I can't really recall."

Darby thought about Gabe's accent, with its trace of French, but she couldn't think of anything she could say that Nan might understand.

They walked around to the front and out through the rusty iron gate.

Nan looked critically at the house. "It's time they fixed this old place up. Fiona tells me the people who bought it come from New Orleans. Perhaps they want to build a lovely safe home here after that last dreadful hurricane."

"Maybe." Darby dropped her skateboard on the road. "Want a try, Nan?" she joked.

Nan didn't look as horrified as Darby thought she would. "Perhaps next time, dear," she said mildly. "I do hope you didn't mind that I gave Shawnie your rock collection."

The rock collection—the one piece of solid evidence that this whole crazy summer might not just have come from her imagination.

Darby smiled at her. "It's okay, Nan. It's better than okay. Did you see the cool *inuksuk* she made me? Way better than some old pile of rocks. It's beautiful."

She coasted slowly beside her grandmother back along Forsyth Street.

"Well, thank goodness for that. Perhaps you can make a new collection when you come back to visit me next year?" Her voice sounded so hopeful.

Darby thought about it for a minute. "Not a bad idea, Nan," she said, with a grin. "I'll probably be ready for a little peace and quiet by next summer. And maybe I'll even get a chance to give Fiona's PlayStation another try."

Nan laughed. "There may be more friends to play with on the street if the new owners have moved in by then. The Island is changing so quickly these days."

"I'm with you, Nan. I like things the way they are." They stopped to look back at the old blue house as the last rays of sun lit up the gingerbread trim in a brilliant golden glow.

The sun must have been playing tricks with Darby's eyes, because for one instant, she was sure she saw a hand, waving cheerily from one of the high gabled windows at the front of the house.

—⁓—

Darby's bags were all packed, and the flashy silver convertible that her father had rented was running in front of the house. No "Taxi by Ernie" ride to the airport, after all. They were all set to take off, but Darby felt a pang of loss surge through her as she hugged Nan goodbye. She held on extra tight for a minute and then kissed Nan's cheek.

"See you next summer, girlie," Nan said.

She turned away to hug Darby's parents, and Darby fiddled with her MP3 player to give herself something else to think about besides going away.

As he helped Darby's mother to get the seatbelt adjusted, her dad leaned across the seat and tugged on the earphone cord. "What do you think, Darby?" he asked, smiling a little. "Would you rather have a brother or a sister?"

"I don't care," Darby said. "But since I'm the only sister the thing will ever have, I think I should get to pick the name. What do you think about Gabriel? That would do for a boy *or* a girl, don'tcha think?"

Everyone muttered approvingly, and Darby looked up the street at the blue house with the gingerbread trim and mentally dusted off her hands. *There you go, Gabe,* she thought. *My job here is done.*

She stared at the sunlight dappling the trees along the street, and thought about all the attention the new baby was getting. What about Gramps? They'd just said goodbye to him. Wasn't he more important than some baby who wasn't even going to show its face for two more months?

But maybe Gramps wouldn't have minded so much. The new baby gave everybody something to look forward to, including Nan. Darby's dad finally got in the car and they all waved a last goodbye and headed up Granville Street to the highway that led to the Confederation Bridge.

"You know, Darby," said her dad. "I'm so happy you agreed with our decision to drive home to Toronto. You still have a couple of weeks before you head back to school, and," he patted her mother's knee, "your mother and I have been talking."

Darby rolled her eyes. All their talking was why she was trying to listen to her music. She sighed and pulled out one earphone.

"We've agreed that it's all very well to visit your relatives," her dad continued in his I-mean-business voice. "But why take an airplane when you have the opportunity to see your country first-hand?" He smiled at his daughter in the rearview mirror. "We've decided it really is about time you got off that skateboard and learned a little bit of the geography and history of your country, don't you think?"

Darby pulled the tiny green polar bear Shawnie had carved out of the pocket of her shorts and rubbed the soft stone under her thumb.

Yeah, Dad. Whatever you say.

Glossary

Abegweit First Nation A First Nations Band in PEI, and also the one of the earliest names given to the Island itself.

Acadian / Acadien Name of a group of settlers, originally from France, who lived in the Maritime provinces, particularly the area now known as Nova Scotia. The Acadian Expulsion by the British (1755–63) meant that people of Acadian descent were forced to move far away from their Maritime home.

Atikuat Innu word for caribou.

Atlée Tlingit word for "Mother."

Bairn "Baby" in Gaelic dialect.

Behemoth A gargantuan object or thing of great power; in this case a printing press being carted across an ocean.

Beothuk Extinct indigenous culture once found on the island of Newfoundland.

Borden Called Borden-Carlton since 1995, now the site of the Confederation Bridge. Previously the docking area for the ferry to new Brunswick.

"Bog boy" / "Filthy Mick" Particularly nasty ways of referring to people of Irish heritage. They refer to the peat bogs of Ireland.

Cenotaph A memorial for people who have died elsewhere—in Canada, these are usually war memorials.

Clout Not (in this case) a punch, but a baby's diaper in Gaelic dialect.

Coffin ship The nickname for ships bringing people to the Americas during times of famine, from the diseases that ran rampant through the starving passengers—typhus, cholera and smallpox among them.

The Colonies / The British Colonies The area (now primarily known as Canada) ceded to Britain in the years after the battle for Quebec, won by the British forces, on the Plains of Abraham in 1759.

Confederation The term given to the forming of the Canadian nation in 1867. The agreement for Confederation was signed in Charlottetown the year before.

Confederation Bridge / The Fixed Link The bridge, nearly 13km long, spanning Northumberland Strait between Prince Edward Island and New Brunswick.

Cur A dog of indeterminate breeding. "Thievin' cur" generally refers to a human being accused of stealing, though some dogs with the innate ability to counter cruise would also qualify.

Da "Dad" in Irish dialect.

Danforth A major street in Toronto's east end, known for excellence in ethnic cuisines, particularly Greek.

Dual trucks Skateboard wheels, often placed closely together to aid in turning stability on downhill runs.

The *Elizabeth* A fictional ship modeled on the coffin ships plying the Atlantic Ocean during the Irish Potato Famine.

"From away" A reference to anyone not born on Prince Edward Island by native-born Islanders.

Flintlock musket A fairly large-bore firearm that used a flint to ignite black powder and fire shot.

Grosse-Île Also known as Grosse Isle, it was an unpopulated island in the St. Lawrence River below Quebec City, and was established as a quarantine station to prevent a cholera epidemic in the British colonies. It was used in the same manner during the Irish Potato Famine to prevent the spread of typhus and smallpox.

The Guardian Charlottetown's Daily Newspaper.

Hearth The base of a fireplace, where the fire is laid upon the hearthstone.

Inuit / Innu Inuit is the name given to the indigenous peoples of the Arctic, including Canada, Alaska, Greenland and Russia. Many of the words used in this story for Darby's trip into pre-history are taken from Inuit (Inuktitut) or from the Innu culture. The Innu encompass the indigenous peoples of the North-east Arctic in Quebec and Labrador. The Tlingit language of the Northwestern Arctic is also represented.

Inuksuk / Inuksuit A pile of rocks used as a landmark or a food cache in the North. (Not to be confused with an Innunguaq, which is a cairn of rocks in roughly human form.)

Irish Potato Famine A great famine in Ireland that began around 1845 and killed more than a million before it was over. It resulted from potato blight, which caused the crop to quickly rot in the ground or in storage. Ireland's absentee farmers fed the mostly poor workforce primarily on potatoes, saving other crops for export and the wealthy. Other potato famines have occurred since, including one in Scotland, but this famine changed the sociological and economic face of Ireland, as many of its people were forced to flee or die.

Kodiak The name of a type of grizzly bear found in the North, particularly in the Kodiak archepelago in Alaska. The largest bear recorded as killed in the North was a Kodiak with a total skull size of 78.1 cm.

Korean War / Korean Conflict A war principally between North and South Korea from 1950–53. Other countries, including Canada, were also involved. American and Soviet involvement in the region helped foster a lead-up to the Cold War.

Lummox An insulting name implying a clumsy, awkward or stupid person.

MicMac / Mi'kmaq First nation from the Maritime region. (Not to be confused with "Mick," which actually refers in a very nasty way to someone's Irish heritage.)

Mirkwood A dense, scary forest from the stories of J.R.R. Tolkien.

Mushum Northern Inuit word for Grandfather.

Nanuq Polar bear in Inuktitut.

Northumberland Strait The part of the Gulf of St. Lawrence that separates Prince Edward Island from the mainland.

Nukum Innu and Northern Cree word for grandma.

Ollie A skateboard manoeuvre in which the boarder jumps, propelling both herself and the board into the air.

Pádraig The Irish form of the name Patrick.

Passenger manifest The list of passengers on board a vessel.

Pestilential Skinny, as if infested with illness or insects, or both.

Petroglyphs Images carved into rock, often associated with prehistoric peoples.

Potato Famine See Irish Potato Famine.

Province House The Provincial Legislature in Charlottetown, Prince Edward Island, Canada's second-oldest seat of government.

Qallupilluq Spirit who lives beneath the ice, in the north. (Quallupilluit refers to three or more spirit.)

Radiant algae Aquatic plants that are bioluminescent (give off a glowing green light). Dinoflagellates (marine plankton) are also bioluminescent.

Rankin Inlet An Inuit hamlet located on the shore of Hudson Bay in Nunuvet.

Sandstone Sedimentary rock composed of highly compressed sand. Principal type of rock found on Prince Edward Island, with a rusty red colour due to the oxidized iron content.

Sháach'i (Sha'achi) A diminutive of Asx'aan Sha'achi, the Tlingit word for sparrow.

Sligo A port town on the west coast of Ireland.

Soapstone Metamorphic rock, with a high content of talc that renders the surface very soft. A common medium for carving by indigenous northern artists.

Smallpox / The pox Highly infectious virus, often fatal if untreated.

St. Lawrence River The waterway connecting the Atlantic Ocean to the first of the Great Lakes, Lake Ontario.

Tuberculosis A disease of the lungs, also known as consumption, fatal if untreated.

Typhus / Typhoid Fever Infectious, often fatal disease, spread through close contact and unclean water.

Wretch A particularly sad or pitiable individual.

Acknowledgements

I spent a lot of summers visiting my own grandparents in PEI, and though this is Darby's story and not mine, a few bits and pieces of my world have lightly dusted hers. Charlottetown and her people have served my imagination richly over the years, and many of her landmarks appear in this story. But there is no Forsyth Street—unless you know the way there, of course; and all the characters in these pages are figments of the warm, summer P.E. Island air.

I'd like to thank all the people who have helped Darby find life in these pages—authors Marsha Skrypuch, Linda Gerber and Kate Coombs, (the usual suspects in my writing world). Thanks also to Michael Hiebert for the loan of Brandon Harris, and to the librarians and archivists at the Confederation Centre Public Library and the Prince Edward Island Public Archives and Records Office. Special thanks for direction and insight into Northern languages and cultures to authors Anita Daher, Richard Van Camp, and Armin Weibe and to

Margaret Anderson, professor of First Nations Studies at the University of Northern British Columbia; Stacie Zaychuk, Manager of the Yukon Beringia Interpretive Centre and John Ritter, founding Director of the Yukon Native Language centre.

Thanks also to my kind and careful editor Amy Black and to my agents Carolyn Swayze and Kris Rothstein for their wisdom and patience.

I would especially like to thank the part of Lucy Maud Montgomery who lives on within the pages of her stories. I grew up wanting to be Anne of Green Gables, deploring my lack of red hair, and cultivating every big, beautiful word I could find. I write these words just about exactly 100 years after Anne first made her appearance, and am living proof that the Island and Lucy Maud continue each to offer their inspiration to readers and writers from Canada and around the world.

Author's Note

A word about Beringia . . .

Darby's adventures are fictional, of course, and take place in a time long before any written record. But in the real world—the world into which Darby's story is woven—the northern reaches of Canada form a vast frontier. This place, so rife with mysterious beauty, has been the subject of much fascination over the years.

Beringia is the name given to a vast, grassy steppe that stretched across from Siberia to North America during the last Ice Age, when many of the world's oceans retreated and were frozen beneath immense sheets of ice. Scientists and historians theorize that the first peoples of North America may have made their way across this region some 24,000 years ago. There is no way of knowing what language these people spoke—it is lost in the mists of history. For the purposes of this story, Darby hears The People use words that come from contemporary Innu, Inuktitut and Tlingit, as a means of honouring some of the many Northern voices that have emerged from the peoples who may have made that tremendous journey so long ago. If you'd like to find out more about this fascinating place, please look for the Study Guide that accompanies this novel at www.kcdyer.com.